'Did anybody ever tell you that you look great in mud?'

'Sorry,' Owen said. 'I'd like to return the compliment, but I can't. You're just not the mud type. Let me help you get it off.'

'No, I don't want your help.'

'Too bad, because I really want to do it.'

It was a primitive form of play, as old as man, as enticing as woman. Winding his hand through her long, wet hair, Owen tugged just hard enough to let her know he could.

Olivia let him draw her back until her gaze met his, only inches separating them. And in that small space where their breath meshed, the air was hot enough to turn the rain to steam...

Available in October 2003 from Silhouette Special Edition

The Cupcake Queen

PATRICIA COUGHLIN

SILHOUETTE®
SPECIAL EDITION™

First published in Great Britain 2003
Silhouette Books, Eton House, 18-24 Paradise Road,
Richmond, Surrey TW9 1SR

© Patricia Madden Coughlin 2002

ISBN 0 373 24454 1

23-1003

Printed and bound in Spain
by Litografia Rosés S.A., Barcelona

PATRICIA COUGHLIN

is a troubling combination of hopeless romantic and dedicated dreamer. Troubling, that is, for anyone hoping to drag her back to the 'real world' when she is in the midst of writing a book. Close family and friends have learned to coexist peacefully with the latest cast of characters in her head. The author of more than twenty-five novels, she has received special recognition from *Publishers Weekly* and *Romantic Times*. Her work also earned her numerous awards, including the prestigious RITA from Romance Writers of America. Patricia lives in Rhode Island, a place very conducive to daydreaming.

For Amy Mullervy,
with gratitude

Chapter One

Olivia hated to lose. To be truthful, it went beyond hate. She abhorred losing, to anyone, under any circumstances, but she especially loathed being bested by one of her four older and frequently infuriating brothers.

Together, they had seen to it that she learned to think fast and stand her ground at a very young age. Now twenty-four, she no longer had to dodge water balloons or check for reptiles before climbing into bed, but their propensity for teasing and practical jokes persisted, and she was adept at deflecting, countering or ignoring their efforts as the situation warranted. Sometimes she even enjoyed the challenge, and she dearly loved her brothers. She just flat-out refused to lose a wager to one of them…particularly as ridiculous a wager as the one she'd allowed herself to be roped into this time.

Olivia winced just thinking about it. If Brad had challenged her privately, she would have found some way to resist the bait. But no, her brother had tossed down the gauntlet in the middle of the Historical Association's annual ball, in front of dozens of amused witnesses. In Baltimore society, it didn't get any more public than that. She'd had no choice but to accept the challenge on the spot, and now pride and her own mulish nature demanded she follow through. Precisely as Brad had anticipated when he set her up, she thought with chagrin.

Pride and pigheadedness. The combination had landed her in a tight spot on more occasions than she cared to recall. But this time she'd even outdone herself. This time she was scaling new heights of absurdity. There certainly was no sane explanation for crawling out of bed at what she deemed the crack of dawn on this brisk October morning, to drive to some godforsaken little town in the backwoods of upstate New York.

She kicked the large suitcase by her side.

"Ouch."

It was packed solid. So solid she'd had to jump up and down on it before she could close the zipper. The "Rules According to Brad" limited her to one suitcase. That presented a formidable challenge to a woman who required a minimum of two bags for a weekend jaunt, and in the end she'd resorted to cheating by wearing everything she couldn't stuff into the suitcase.

There was a reason the layered look went out of style, she reflected, squirming uncomfortably inside a turtleneck jersey, denim shirt and three sweaters. She didn't even want to think about how she must look. Not that it was likely to matter much where she was headed. For all she knew, the layered look was still the rage in Danby.

She reached for the oversize tote bag which she defied Brad to call a second suitcase and was rummaging through it for a map when her mother joined her in the foyer of Twin Brooks, the grand Georgian-style mansion that had been home to the Ashfields for nearly a century.

"What time do you expect Bradford?" Helen Ashfield asked her youngest, and most exasperating, child.

"I told him I was leaving at ten sharp and he's supposed to be here to see me off. Which gives him—" Olivia glanced at her watch "—five minutes. Damn, why didn't I think to stipulate that if he isn't here on time, he forfeits?"

"Perhaps because you were too busy making a spectacle of yourself, throwing arrows…"

"I think you mean darts."

"Of course, *darts,*" her mother conceded, oozing disapproval. "That makes it infinitely more dignified than tossing *arrows* at a map stuck to the wall of the Continental Ballroom."

Olivia shrugged. "It seemed the most logical way to choose a destination under the circumstances."

"Logical? Logical? There is not one scintilla of logic in this latest… escapade that you and your brother have cooked up." She sighed. "I thought Bradford had more sense."

"Well, he doesn't." It did not escape Olivia that her mother had not said that she thought *she* had more sense.

"Does that mean you are obligated to go along with whatever asinine scheme he proposes?"

"What can I say? He has a way of bringing out the worst of my inner child."

"Please don't joke, Olivia. Your father and I are very worried about you going off alone like this."

"Mom, I've been traveling alone for years."

"Traveling, yes. Not living and working and fending for yourself in some strange place. I cannot for the life of me understand why— Don't say it." She raised her palm to halt Olivia's response. "I'm weary of hearing you say it's the principle of the matter…whatever that means. How principle can be at stake in such a foolish, not to mention dangerous, stunt, eludes me."

"We're not talking about Beirut, Mom. I'm going to a town named Danby, population 14,000, for heaven's sake. I suspect the crime rate there is lower than in Baltimore."

"I don't care what the population is. Every one of them is a stranger. And it's not as if you'll be spending a weekend. You'll be there for months…"

"Eight weeks."

"Alone, with no family, no job, no friends, no one who even knows who you are, for heaven's sake."

"That's the point," Olivia countered wryly, bringing a familiar, long-suffering expression to her mother's face.

The sunlight streaming through the leaded glass windows of the foyer might have been hard on the appearance of another woman in her fifties, but not Helen Templeton Ashfield. A combination of good genes and good sense resulted in a softly glowing complexion, a still-slim and strong body and golden-brown hair, cut to flatter her classic features and draw attention to her brilliant blue eyes. The fact that the softly layered style was the look of the moment mattered not at all to her mother, who had a remarkable talent for knowing what was right for her...in hairstyles and in life.

Olivia liked to think she'd inherited those gifts. There was no question she had done all right in the looks department. Blond, blue-eyed and willowy, she was aware she could turn heads dressed in baggy sweats. Not that she would ever be caught dead in them. Her style was one she'd dubbed "casual glam," and she wore it well. She clung to the belief that hidden somewhere inside her—deep inside—she possessed the same instinct for more significant matters. It was just taking her a while to dig it out.

She was convinced that when she at last found whatever it was she was meant to do with her life, she would know it instantly, the way her mother insisted she had known her future the very first time she'd set eyes on Richard Ashfield. She was definitely narrowing the field of possibilities. Through trial and error she had established she was *not* destined to work with young children or stay cooped up in an office all day or work around chemicals, especially those of a combustible nature. And she'd yet to set sight on a man and know for sure that she'd want to spend a weekend with him, much less "till death did them part."

Her mother was still voicing her objections. Taking a deep breath, Olivia decided she would try one more time to make her understand what she was about to do. "Mom, the reason I'm going to Danby is precisely *because* I don't know a soul there, to prove that I can survive completely on my own. With...how did my dear brother put it? No trust account..."

"No credit cards. No Daddy," interrupted a masculine voice from behind her.

"Ah, the devil himself," Olivia drawled, turning.

Brad Ashfield, like all the Ashfield men, was tall and athletic and heartbreakingly handsome. He grinned at his only sister and moved to give his mother a quick kiss on her cheek. "Good morning, Mother. Great day for a drive in the country, wouldn't you say?"

Rubbing his hands together like the villain in a cartoon, he glanced from Olivia's unsmiling face to the suitcase beside her and nodded approvingly. "One bag. See? You can follow orders. You're even ready on time. Hell, Liv, if you keep this up, you just might last more than two days on a real job after all."

"Oh, I intend to last more than two days. I intend to last the entire eight weeks. There's nothing I wouldn't do for the pleasure of seeing you shave your head in public."

"That would be a sight to draw a crowd, all right," Brad agreed. Looking smug, he added, "Why, I'll bet it would be nearly as big a crowd as we're going to have when you shave yours."

Her mother swung her horrified gaze to Olivia. "Oliv-ia, please tell me you are not going to—"

"I am not going to shave my head in public or anywhere else, Mother. I fully intend to win this bet. This victory will be my swan song, my final participation in anything my brothers dream up, proving once and for all that nothing my conniving, eavesdropping, interfering…"

Brad looked indignant. "I did not eavesdrop. I was simply dancing in close proximity to you and that Taylor guy when I happened to overhear you reeling him in with that old line about how you dreamed of running away from your unbearably tedious life of wealth and privilege and make your own way in the world." He

•

shook his head with mock dismay. "Really, Liv, I should have thought you'd retired that one years ago."

"I believe 'find myself' was the phrase I used," she informed him.

"Yes, of course. I remember thinking it was such a charmingly retro expression."

"Did you think that right before you barged into my private conversation for the sole purpose of taunting me and backing me into a corner in public?"

"That's not my recollection at all," he said, stroking his chin with such phony sincerity that Olivia's lip curled. "I only recall chatting with my sister and her partner after inadvertently bumping into them on the dance floor."

"Inadvertently, my eye," she muttered.

"After that I simply did my best to encourage you to follow your dream…you know, that lifelong dream of finding yourself. Hell, a lot of brothers wouldn't even care that their kid sister was lost, never mind go to all this trouble to help her find herself. Seems to me you should be thanking me, not finding fault with every little—"

"Thanking you?" she snapped, tossing back thick, straight blond hair that fell past her shoulders. "You're lucky I didn't—"

"Stop! Both of you." Their mother silenced them with a look that had shriveled braver souls. "You make me wish I could still send you to your rooms for a time-out."

Olivia and Brad chuckled at their mother's exasperation, and even she surrendered to a small smile edged with regret.

"But I can't," she continued, all business once again.

"I can still threaten and nag, however, and I shall. Olivia, are you determined to go through with this?"

"Very," she replied.

"In that case, Bradford, carry your sister's suitcase to the car."

He lifted it with some effort. "What do you have in here?" he grumbled. "Cement blocks?"

"Wouldn't you like to know?" she retorted. "You said one bag. That's one bag. What's in it is none of your business."

"I'll go along with that. And to prove what a good sport I am, I won't even ask whether you packed on a few pounds overnight or you're wearing enough to clothe an entire softball team."

Olivia smiled at him. "Have I told you how much I'm going to miss you?"

"Actually, you haven't," countered her brother.

"This much," she snapped, pressing the tip of her thumb and forefinger tightly together.

He laughed all the way out the door. Olivia linked arms with her mother as they followed.

"You have to promise to call," said her mother.

"I will, Mom, I promise."

"Every day."

"Probably not every day. It's long-distance and I'll be paying my own phone bill. But I will definitely call as often as I can."

Accepting that reluctantly, her mother continued. "And I want you to promise me you will be careful and not take risks of any nature."

"No risks. You have my word. Trust me, if it was adventure I was looking for I wouldn't be going to Danby."

"And I also want your word that no matter what the

final outcome of this, you will not, under any circumstances—''

''Shave my head? Trust me, Mom, do you think I'd have agreed to this if I thought there was the slightest possibility I could lose?''

Helen Ashfield searched her daughter's eyes. ''You wouldn't have?''

Olivia shook her head, slipped on her sunglasses and grinned. ''Not a chance. Think about it, Mom, all I have to do is find a job and support myself for eight weeks.''

The color seemed to drain from her mother's face. ''Oh, dear.''

''Don't worry,'' she said, hiding a trace of annoyance as she hugged her mother. ''It'll be a piece of cake.''

Maybe Brad was doing her a favor, she thought as she started down the brick steps to the wide circular drive. She was pretty tired of being the family ''joke.'' Good old Olivia, beautiful, but…basically useless. An intelligent woman but a pretty ornament. Well, they were all wrong. Just because she hadn't discovered what she wanted to do with her life didn't mean she was destined to do nothing. She was perfectly capable of doing anything she set her mind to, and she was about to prove it.

''Whoa. That's not my car,'' she told Brad as he swung her bag into the trunk of a white sedan parked behind her car.

''Of course it's not,'' he agreed cheerfully, closing the trunk. ''You can't use your car for the next eight weeks.''

''Why not?''

''Because it would violate the terms of our agreement.''

''There was no mention of cars in our agreement.''

"Sure there was," he countered. "It falls under 'trappings.' We agreed you would not take with you any outward trappings of your true identity that might raise questions. That," he continued, pointing at her beloved silver Jaguar, "is definitely an outward trapping."

"And you," retorted Olivia as she snatched the keys he was dangling before her, "are definitely a petty, devious jerk."

Enduring the dents and scrapes and mismatched wheel covers, she slid behind the wheel of the used sedan and slammed the door. The seat felt too big for her. The whole car felt too big for her. Compared to her sleek, low-slung Jag it was like driving a bus. When the engine sputtered, she said a prayer that it wouldn't start, but it did, and after only a few jerky stops as she experimented with the unfamiliar brakes, she was on her way…with Brad's final words ringing in her ears.

"Don't forget your weekly check-ins, sweetheart."

Chapter Two

"I'm so glad you called, Olivia. It's a relief just to hear your voice."

"Yours, too," Olivia replied, surprised just how good it was to hear a familiar voice. Had it really been only a little more than a week?

"I can't talk long," she explained to her mother. "I splurged on one of those prepaid phone cards and I don't want to use all thirty minutes on one call."

Helen Ashfield sighed. "Really, Olivia. I can send you more phone cards. For that matter, why don't I just drop a check in—"

"Mom…"

"Discreetly, of course."

"Don't you dare! I vowed to do this on my own and I intend to." She kept the "or die trying" part to herself. "Which brings me to the other reason I can't talk long. I'm calling you from work."

"Work? Are you sure?"

"Oh ye of little faith," she retorted, not entirely joking. "Of course I'm sure. You happen to be speaking with the receptionist for one of the busiest doctors in Danby."

"A doctor." Pause. "Do you really think that's wise? With your limited experience, I mean."

"Relax, Mom. Dr. Allison Black, better known around here as Doc Allison, is a vet. I'm working at the Danby Animal Hospital."

"I suppose that's not quite as risky," her mother said. "Just the same, be careful in what have been your problem areas in the past, relaying messages, showing up on the right day, that sort of thing."

"I'll be sure to do that, Mother," she said, drumming her fingers on the desktop calendar advertising heart worm medication. "But so far everything is going pretty smoothly."

"Is today your first day?"

Her grip tightened on the receiver. "Actually I've worked nearly every day since I arrived." That was almost true. Just not on the same job.

"I can't wait to tell your father. He'll be amazed."

"Just don't tell Brad. I want that pleasure so I can hear him start to sweat."

Her mother chuckled. "All right. Not a word to your brother. Now tell me all about your job."

"There's not a lot to tell. I answer the phone, schedule appointments, check in patients, that sort of thing."

"It sounds very…busy," her mother said brightly.

"It's busy, all right, but repetitive. If you don't hear from me again you can assume I've died of boredom…or else run off with a veterinary pharmaceutical salesman. Don't laugh. That's what the last receptionist did and I'm beginning to understand why. It was a lucky break for me, though, since Doc Allison was desperate and I was the only applicant.''

''I see. Well, your father always says you have to start somewhere.''

''He also says things like 'A bird in the hand is worth two in the bush.'''

''True.'' She paused a few seconds. ''Olivia?''

''Yes?''

''Now that we have the forced good cheer out of the way, how are you *really?*''

Olivia sighed. ''You're good, you know, very, very good…even over long distances.''

''I know. I've had considerable practice. Let's hear it.''

''Off the record?''

''Of course.''

''I'm miserable, that's how I am. First I couldn't find a job, then when I finally found one—waiting tables at the local diner—they made me wear this hideous uniform with a pink ruffled apron—you know how I feel about pink—and I ended up pouring a pot of hot coffee on some guy's head and getting fired my very first day.''

''Why on earth did you pour coffee on the man?''

''Because he grabbed my butt, that's why, and then all the other men at the table started hooting and laughing and I saw red. Before I knew it, I was standing there holding an empty pot. Actually it was only half-full to start with, and it wasn't all that hot, either.''

''And those meanies fired you, anyway? Imagine that.''

''Very funny.''

"Olivia, sweetheart, I could have told you that you're not cut out to be a waitress."

"I wasn't looking at it as a career move. Besides, when you don't know what you *are* cut out for, one job looks as good as another."

"Mmm. That must explain how someone who's never been, shall we say, overly fond of animals finds herself working for a veterinarian."

"I don't *dislike* animals," she protested. "Not completely anyway. Only the shedding, smelling, drooling stuff. I give to the SPCA and I wouldn't be caught dead in real fur. Heck, I was even a vegetarian once. Remember the summer I turned fifteen?"

"Vividly. Did you tell them all that to get the job?"

"More or less." Silence. "All right, I lied through my teeth and said I adored animals and that I have extensive office experience working for my dear departed veterinarian uncle whose records were destroyed in a fire."

"Olivia, when are you going to learn…?"

"Soon. Word of honor. Right now I have to focus on surviving the next six and a half weeks."

"Is this job really going smoothly or was that bravado, as well?"

"Half and half. Yesterday was pretty rough. I accidentally left this Doberman with an infected tear duct parked in the waiting room for more than an hour. Of course, I didn't *know* it was infected, much less that it was so serious he had to be rushed to a veterinary ophthalmologist."

"I gather your late uncle didn't treat too many infected tear ducts," her mother remarked in a dry tone.

"That's not helpful, Mom. Do you want to hear this or not?"

"Of course."

"Well, the good news is old Bozo isn't going to lose his eye after all. That's the dog's name. Bozo."

"I see. And the bad news?"

"Doc Allison was furious and made me promise to actually look at the patients at check-in and alert her to any glaring abnormalities. *And* she put me on notice that another incident will force her to let me go."

"Oh, she did, did she?"

Olivia smiled, not surprised her mother was personally offended by the warning. It was perfectly fine for *her* to question her daughter's ability, but even a hint of outside criticism elicited her maternal ire.

"A bit overbearing, isn't she? This is your first week on the job, after all."

"True, but at the time she was still pretty upset over the hedgehog." She decided not to mention the mix-up with the fish tank, since in all fairness no one had bothered to tell her that the coral was living, not plastic, and had some sort of super sensitivity to sudden changes in its environment.

"Hedgehog?" her mother repeated warily, as if the word itself were dangerous.

"Yes. I sat on him. Not intentionally. He was the one curled up in *my* chair, after all. And I didn't come down with my full weight...not once I felt those damned spikes. The little rodent totally lost it just the same. For all the noise and running around you would think it was *my* spikes that had punched holes in *his* favorite slacks...not to mention a pair of those silk panties I like so much—the ones I have to order from that little shop in Paris."

"Olivia, this is so comical it's tragic. I'm worried about you."

"Don't be. That was yesterday," she reminded her, trying to sound reassuring as she absently swiveled her chair so she was gazing out the window, her back to the entrance. "So far today I haven't slipped up once."

"It isn't even noon."

Olivia sank back in her chair. "Don't remind me."

"You're groaning because you know I'm right. I insist you stop this nonsense before you or one of those poor animals really gets hurt, and come home."

"No."

"Honey, I'm certain your brother will understand and—"

"No. Not a chance."

Her mother huffed impatiently. "Really, Olivia. Why can't you be reasonable just this once?"

"Because I'm not a wuss, that's why, and because I don't go back on my word, and," she continued, her voice rising to match her irritation, "because I'd rather walk the plank—naked—than give that sneaky devil the satisfaction of seeing me shave my head in public."

A snicker from behind was Olivia's first clue someone had walked in without her hearing and was standing close enough to hear every word she said.

She whispered, "Love you. Gotta go," and swiveled around to hang up the phone and grab the day's schedule book.

"Sorry to keep you waiting," she said, plastering her best receptionist smile in place as she looked up—way up—and straight into a pair of dark, deep-set gray eyes she'd seen only once before and would not soon forget.

"Because he grabbed my butt," she'd told her mother. "Because the other men all laughed," she'd told her. What she hadn't told her was how the man hadn't even flinched when she tossed the coffee at him, and how his dark, unsmiling gaze had caught and held hers for what seemed like forever, until it was somehow understood between them that he was good and ready to look away, and let her do the same. She also hadn't mentioned how, with the front of his shirt and faded jeans soaked with coffee, he had paid for his breakfast, laid a five-dollar tip on the table and walked out…all without saying a word.

His absolute control had unsettled her in a way his insolence couldn't possibly. She was an old hand at dealing with unwanted male attention. She was not, however, accustomed to allowing a man to throw her off balance. And she didn't like it. The fact that he was some hick from Danby made it more maddening. As soon as she'd handed in her apron, she had put him out of her mind. Or tried to at least.

"Well, well," he murmured finally, the sardonic slant of his mouth leaving no doubt he remembered their last meeting as vividly as she did.

How much of her phone conversation had he overheard? Probably too much, given her recent streak of things going from bad to worse. She waited for him to speak first, but he was preoccupied with studying her, his hooded gaze cool and utterly unfathomable. The rest of him, on the other hand, was easy to read.

He was a big man, not heavy, just big—tall and broad-shouldered and solidly muscled. His face was suntanned, suggesting he worked outdoors. His scraped knuckles and rough hands told Olivia he worked with those hands and worked hard. A glance at the dark-brown hair curling around his ears and collar and she knew there were lots of things he'd rather do with his time than sit in a barber's chair. She had a hunch he didn't like sitting around of any kind.

His mouth was generous enough to be intriguing, his cheekbones high, his jaw solid…and stubborn. She supposed the town's female population considered him quite handsome, in that primitive, diamond-in-the-rough way some women found irresistible. Personally, she'd never understood the appeal of a "fixer-upper," in houses or men.

What she found most revealing about him, however, was something more subtle than the rest. Actually, it was two things. The way he moved and the way he was still. This, she decided, was a man totally and unmistakably at ease in his own skin. It was the sort of intrinsic confidence you couldn't buy. If you could, most of the men she knew would have it. It also wasn't easily cultivated. Few people cared to turn over rocks inside themselves; fewer still could come to terms with what they were and were not.

Of course, the fact that this particular man was so self-accepting indicated he was also an appallingly bad judge of character.

While she was taking stock of him, he continued to look at her long and hard. Knock yourself out, thought Olivia, buoyed by her own rush of confidence. This was familiar ground. Stares and admiring male glances were a fact of life. Also a fact of life was her skill at keeping hormone-driven responses in check, even when the man had other ideas.

Another of her father's favorite quotes was "Use the gifts God gave you." It wasn't too long after puberty struck that she figured out her greatest God-given gift was the one she came face-to-face with when she looked in a mirror. It was a little while before she was comfortable with the ardent attention it brought her, and longer still until she claimed the power that was part of the package. Once she had, beauty became her weapon of choice, and through trial and error she'd come to wield it with finesse.

If this small-town Don Juan thought he could rattle her twice in one lifetime, he was sorely mistaken.

"What is it with you, lady?" he asked, when he appeared to have looked his fill at last. His tone was cordial, gentle even, but his voice was deep, the gravelly kind of deep that could give a woman goose bumps if she let it. "Are you flat-out crazy?"

"What makes you ask?" she countered coolly.

"Oh, I don't know, something about you dumping coffee on strangers and wanting to walk a plank naked."

"Oh, that. Yes, I'm flat-out crazy."

Their eyes met. He might have a bigger Adam's apple than she did, but she had a few assets of her own— a sub-Arctic tone and a dismissive gaze that had cut the machismo out from under inebriated frat boys and philandering Fortune 500 executives alike. The combination had never failed her.

Until now.

For the first time in her life she brought it to bear full force on a man and nothing happened. No stuttering or shifting of feet, and not so much as a flicker of embarrassment.

Concentrate, she told herself, allowing her lips to curve into a subtly amused smile. Next to public rejection, men most hated being laughed at.

"Now it's my turn to ask you a question," she said. "Do you cop a feel off every waitress who slaps a $1.99 special in front of you? Or is it only crazy ladies you can't keep your hands off?"

First he laughed. Then he stepped around the chest-high counter separating the entry and office, and planted his palms in the center of her desk. An ancient leather bomber jacket hung open over his black sweater and jeans. He was also sporting several days' black stubble, and she would bet an extra week in Danby that if she bothered to check out his feet, she'd see some battered member of the boot family. The complete "bad boy" ensemble. Generations of self-proclaimed rebels had adopted it to affect a menacing, misunderstood look, with an undercurrent of raw sexuality.

And for good reason, she acknowledged to herself. It worked. As he continued to lean forward slowly, Olivia subdued the urge to wheel her chair out of reach.

"I think I'll keep you guessing about my taste in women," he said, his too deep voice now also too close. "I will tell you this much. If I ever do decide to put my hands on you, I'll make damn sure you know who it is touching you. I'm scared as hell you'll get spooked again and hurl something really lethal at me."

Funny, he didn't look scared. He looked pretty damned amused, Olivia decided, bristling. "Let's get something straight. I didn't throw coffee at you because I was spooked. The truth is, I wasn't even upset," she added, shrugging. "It was strictly a matter of principle."

"Yeah?" The corners of his wide mouth curled upward. "What principle is that?"

"The one that says a man keeps his hands to himself unless I invite him to do otherwise."

His grin became full-blown. "Unless? Or until? Either way, lady, you've got yourself a deal."

"Lucky me," she murmured, taking the hand he extended to seal the bargain. It wouldn't have surprised her in the least if he turned out to be a fast-fingered

Harry as well as a groper. The tags were from her college days, when she and a small group of close friends would pigeonhole a man according to his most impressive—or offensive—quality. Instead of prolonging the handshake, however, or rubbing a finger suggestively against her palm, he shook her hand in crisp, businesslike fashion and let go.

It was a little like being dismissed and she wouldn't have let him get away with it if Doc Allison hadn't come charging into the room in her usual rush.

Her boss was in her thirties, a trim brunette with a no-nonsense manner and a habit of doing at least two things at once. Now she continued scribbling notes on a chart, slapped a list on the desk and began talking to Olivia.

"Do you think you can find these medications in the stockroom? And please rummage up some vitamin samples to give to Honey-Bunch's mom when she checks out."

"Right away." With no small amount of pleasure, Olivia aimed a lofty look at the man in front of her. "I'm afraid it's going to be a few minutes before I can check you in."

She got to her feet slowly, certain he was like most men and wouldn't be able to resist checking out those parts of her that had been hidden under the desk. At this point even that small, pseudo-victory would make her feel better.

"Don't bother," he replied to her comment about the wait. Not only did he ignore the chance to check her out more thoroughly, but he turned away, shifting his attention to the vet, who had stopped writing and looked up at the sound of his voice.

She immediately broke into a friendly smile. "Hey, stranger. I didn't know you were here."

"You asked me to stop by, remember?"

"Of course. But you're way early."

Curious, Olivia lingered by her desk, shuffling papers for as long as she dared. It was long enough to note that his return smile was also friendly, as opposed to the nasty smirk he'd used on her.

"I finished setting up that new trail sooner than I expected," he was saying. "If this is bad timing, Doc—"

"Not at all," she assured him, taking his arm and tugging him along with her through the Staff Only doorway that led to her private office. The ease with which he fell in step with the other woman was not lost on Olivia. "I'm anxious to have you take a look at…"

That was the last thing she heard before the door swung shut.

What? Take a look at what? She resisted the urge to stamp her foot. Telling herself she really wasn't interested in his reason for being there, or anything else about the man, she got busy gathering the medications on the list, presenting them to the furry little dog's "mom" and recording payment for the visit.

As soon as the woman and dog left, she headed for the bathroom, or, more accurately, the mirror over the bathroom sink. Wishing it were full length, she inspected herself from a variety of angles. She looked fine, she decided. Better than fine. She looked the way she always looked, like herself. Obviously, if there was a problem, it wasn't hers. Not that she'd been concerned otherwise. Merely curious. Mildly curious. Blame it on boredom.

Just the same, she took time to remove her lipstick

and reapply it. She also combed her hair, then bent at the waist, tossing it forward and back to lose that just-combed look. Men were suckers for tousled hair and for anything else that helped link women and bed in their thoughts. Last, she pulled a tiny gold perfume atomizer from her bag and gave herself a quick spray of Sultry, rubbing the back of her wrists together until the scent of the aptly named perfume drifted over her.

She inhaled deeply. There, that was better. Strictly speaking, the perfume violated the terms of the wager. Sultry was French and hideously expensive by anyone's standards. It was also worth every last penny, and she wasn't going to lose a minute's sleep over what Brad would say if he knew she'd smuggled it along.

If she'd freshened up for the benefit of Doc Allison's visitor—which she assured herself she had not—it was a wasted effort. Either he was a very fast looker or he had left the back way. She would like to think he'd ducked out the back to avoid another round with her, but she was too good a judge of character. Nothing about him suggested he was a man who shied away from confrontation.

Perhaps his choice of exits had to do with whatever Doc Allison had invited him to see in her private sanctum. Hmm, that had definite possibilities. Her boss was married, happily so by all appearances, but she sure wouldn't swoon from shock to discover *he* was overstepping his bounds.

"Typical tomcat," she muttered.

A hissing sound drew Olivia's attention to the carrier she was using for a footrest. A pair of yellow eyes stared accusingly at her from within. After what just happened, she should know better than to sound off without checking first to see who was in earshot. She'd forgotten all about Izzy, the black cat with a bandaged paw who was supposed to have been picked up over an hour ago.

"Sorry, pal, I call 'em as I see 'em," she said. "But I don't blame you for being offended at being lumped together with that guy."

Izzy's stare didn't waver. If she were the type who spooked easily, this would do it. She even went as far as to shift her feet to the floor and nudge the gray plastic carrier a few inches away.

"Nice cat," she said. "Good kitty. Mommy will be here any minute."

The cat countered with something between a hiss and a growl, and batted his bandaged front paw against the wire screen of the carrier.

"Cut it out, Izzy," she ordered. "I've heard all about your 'wonder cat' routine, answering the phone and opening your carrier door and, well, frankly, Iz, I think it's a load of bull." She ignored the growl that rumbled from the cat's throat. "Just the same, the last thing I need right now is for you to rip off your bandage or hurt yourself on my watch. So cut it out."

The cat pawed harder.

Olivia tapped the door with her toe. "What's the matter, Izzy? Don't you speak English? How about French?" she inquired. *"Touche pas. Assis."*

So much for her brothers' claim that a degree in French culture was useless.

"What in God's name are you doing now?"

Gretchen, Doc's assistant, had come to retrieve the next patient's chart. She stood with it in her hand, watching Olivia, who smiled at her to no avail. Gretchen was nineteen, a little on the plump side, and from the start she'd eyed Olivia as if expecting her to make off with a case of flea collars any second.

"Izzy was clawing the latch with his front paw, and I didn't want him to hurt himself," she explained.

"So you kicked him?" Gretchen shook her head. "Figures, after that stunt yesterday."

"Yesterday was a mistake," she pointed out. "I've apologized at least a dozen times. And I wasn't kicking anything. I was trying to get the cat to stop picking at the latch."

"Maybe he wants to get out of that carrier."

Olivia couldn't resist returning the girl's smug smile. "I'm sure that's exactly what he wants. Unfortunately for old Izzy here, his owner didn't opt for the deluxe visit, you know, the one that includes roaming privileges whenever the mood strikes him."

"Maybe he's in the mood to use the litter box," Gretchen retorted, speaking slowly, as if Olivia were not too bright. "Did you ever consider that?"

"Not directly," she conceded. "Not yet, anyway." She looked around. "Where's the litter—?"

Before she'd finished the question, Gretchen was pointing toward the door at the back of the building, where the operating and recovery rooms were located. "You can't miss it," she said, turning to go.

"But what if once he's out of the carrier he doesn't want to get back in?" Olivia called after her, ignoring the look of disgust Gretchen tossed over her shoulder. "What if he runs outside?"

"He's an indoor cat," the younger woman called before disappearing into an examining room.

An indoor cat. She had a vague recollection from somewhere that indoor cats were indoor cats because they'd been declawed. Or the other way around. Whichever, knowing it gave her confidence as she pushed the carrier closer to the door Gretchen had indicated and opened the latch.

"Go ahead. Go. *Va,* Izzy. Do whatever it is you need to do," she urged.

That's all the prodding Izzy needed to sweep from the carrier and, with a regal lack of concern for anyone else's agenda, sit and begin to groom himself.

"Move it, Izzy," she said, "This is no time for a sponge bath."

The phone rang.

"Damn," she muttered, glancing at the phone, then at Izzy, then back at the phone. "That's it. Time's up. Back in the carrier."

She held open the carrier door and reached for Izzy. The cat bolted. He was on the desk, over the counter and headed for the exit before she could say "Bad luck."

Ignoring the phone, Olivia went after him, scrambling over the counter without Izzy's grace or agility. For a cat with a bum paw, he was damned fast. She swerved around a woman holding a white poodle and collided instead with a young man on his way in.

"I'm Dan," he said at the sight of her name tag. "I'm here to pick up the vaccine for—"

"I'll be right with you," she said without breaking stride.

Izzy was sitting at the edge of the parking lot, watching for Olivia with those yellow eyes. She approached him slowly, desperate that this not mushroom into a full-blown "incident." There was no way she was going to let some gimp-legged cat screw things up.

Praying Izzy couldn't distinguish a sincere human

smile from a phony one, she cooed, "Nice cat. Sweet cat."

Izzy purred, and waited until she was within arm's reach before spinning and disappearing into the bushes that were along the side of the building.

Cursing, she took off after him.

She emerged on the other side with scratches on her face and leaves in her hair, and found herself in a narrow clearing between the animal hospital and the ancient wooden contraption that was home to Allison's beehives.

She spotted Izzy a half second before she saw the snake. Again the cat was faster. He already had his back arched and was hissing with such venom the snake shot through the grass straight toward Olivia.

She shouted and made a wild leap in the air with no thought as to where she might land. On the way down her shoulder slammed into something solid, sending her sprawling backward. The hives, she thought, the instant she landed and immediately scrambled to her feet. Before she could assess the damage, there was a muffled, almost eerie sound in the shady clearing, and then suddenly the air was filled with bees. Black with them. Honeybees. Seven hundred and fifty dollars worth of honeybees to be exact. The invoice had arrived in the mail that very morning.

Cursing as passionately as she ever had, she plunged back into the bushes. The bees swarmed above and were waiting for her in the parking lot. She ran for the closest shelter, a pickup truck, and climbed inside, quickly rolling up the window. It was only when she reached to roll up the window on the driver's side that she realized she wasn't alone. A dog as big as a bear sat behind the wheel.

As he looked at her, he dropped his lower jaw, and the sight of all those big white teeth made Olivia decide to take her chances with the bees. She opened the door, but before she could jump out, the dog plowed over her. Slamming the door behind him, she grabbed a newspaper to whack the bees that had made it inside. When she'd gotten them all, she stuffed paper into the vents and took her first good look at the scene outside.

"Oh, no," she breathed, recognizing the young man she'd run into minutes earlier. He was spinning in circles, waving his baseball cap in a frantic attempt to protect himself and the huge black dog from the onslaught of bees. The dog stood his ground by the man's side, barking and shaking his huge head.

Olivia grabbed the newspaper and was getting out to join the fray when Allison appeared brandishing a fire extinguisher. She motioned for Olivia to stay put. Gretchen came from the other side of the building, armed with a hose, and together they fired on the swarm, allowing the man and dog to make it inside and then somehow managing to turn the tide of bees until the air was only dotted with a persistent few.

Gretchen remained on guard with the hose, while Allison dropped the fire extinguisher and hurried inside, pausing only long enough to glare at Olivia.

Even with her minimal work experience she could tell it did not look good.

Her hunch only grew stronger when a rescue vehicle and fire engine careened into the parking lot with sirens blaring. A troop of firefighters clad in black boots and red rubber coats disembarked. A stretcher was rushed inside.

Olivia followed. As she passed Gretchen, the girl shook her head.

"Another *accident?*" she drawled.

"As a matter of—"

"Save your breath. You're going to need it to talk Owen out of killing you with his bare hands. My guess is he'll be here any second now."

"Okay, I'll bite," countered Olivia. "Who's Owen?"

Gretchen smirked. "Owen Rancourt? Just about the most hard-assed, hard-driving trainer anywhere, that's who. That's dog trainer," she added with an air of superiority. "As in security, and search and rescue. Danny Dewar is Owen's right-hand man, and Romeo is his all-time number-one dog. And thanks to you they're both in there covered with beestings."

Olivia could feel a headache coming on. A real doozy of one.

"Some people die from beestings," Gretchen informed her.

"And some are strangled because they don't know when to keep their mouths shut," she snapped. "Would you like to guess which is more likely to be your fate?"

Gretchen's response was lost in a sudden flurry of activity as Danny was rushed to the rescue vehicle on the stretcher. From the looks of it, he was already hooked up to oxygen and an IV. Olivia's stomach clenched painfully. She may not have meant for any of this to happen, but it happened just the same and she alone was to blame. It was like a bad joke. She was in Danby to prove to everyone—maybe even to herself— that she was more than a beautiful, essentially useless ornament, suited only to decorate some rich man's life. Instead she was piling up proof that not only was she useless, she was downright dangerous. Men, hedgehogs, for pity's sake, even *bees* weren't safe around her.

As much as she hated to admit it, maybe her mother was right. If she had heeded her mother's advice, she would be on her way home right now and no one would be suffering because of her ineptitude. Doc Allison would still have her treasured hives, poor Danny wouldn't be swollen and blotchy and strapped to a stretcher, and Owen Rancourt, whoever the hell he was, wouldn't be on his way there to "kill her with his bare hands," as Gretchen had put it. That was probably a slight exaggeration, but even if the prediction proved dead-on, she didn't have it in her to put up much of a fight.

Gretchen went inside, leaving her alone to watch the rescue vehicle drive away. When it reached the road, the driver was forced to stop by a gleaming black-and-chrome pickup, whose driver seemed hell-bent on making the turn into the parking lot. She continued to watch as the truck pulled parallel to the rescue vehicle and stopped so the two drivers could converse briefly. Then the rescue vehicle continued on and the truck shot toward her with enough speed to spray gravel.

Even before it came to a complete stop, Olivia knew the menacing-looking truck belonged to Owen Rancourt. Call it intuition. Call it inevitable. Call it the fitting end to what threatened to be the worst day of her entire useless life.

Hell, call it plain old bad luck. The facts didn't change.

Fact one: judging from the expression on the man's face as he jumped from his truck and caught sight of her, Gretchen had called it exactly. Owen Rancourt had murder in his eye.

Fact two: she and Owen the Horrible had tangled before.

Twice.

Chapter Three

For the first time since the frantic call summoning him there, Owen's adrenaline level began to level off. Not that it was apparent from the way his truck ripped across the paved lot. Whatever relief he felt was a result of seeing for himself that Dan, his only full-time employee and damn near his only close friend in the world, was in good hands and on his way to the hospital. Now he needed to see Romeo. Even within that small circle Owen counted as friends, Romeo stood alone.

It was the general belief in town that Owen Rancourt preferred dogs to people. It was not an impression he went out of his way to contradict. He wasn't one of those activists who ranked animal rights equal to those of humans. It was simply a fact that, much of the time, he'd rather be in the company of his dogs than most people he knew. And if that little quirk in his nature prompted others to keep their distance, well, that was just fine with him.

There was a long list of reasons he favored dogs. High on that list was that they never trapped him into making small talk, or asked questions about things that were none of their business, or demanded more than he was willing or able to give at that moment. A passing scratch behind the ears or an hour of throwing a Frisbee, a good dog received both with a wagging tail and single-minded devotion.

Loyalty. That was also near the top of his list. Right up there with predictability. Once a dog was properly trained and bonded with his handler, you could count on him doing his job, doing his *best*, every time out. No surprises. No hesitation. No second-guessing. And his dogs could count on him the very same way. Simple and straightforward. That's the way he liked things, and he did everything in his power to keep his life working that way.

There had been nothing simple or straightforward about the phone call some babbling pet owner had made on Doc Allison's behalf. Even now he wasn't sure what the hell had happened. The rescue crew had only taken enough time to tell him Danny's vital signs were almost back to normal and he should be all right once they got him to the hospital. All he had been able to decipher from the phone call was what sounded like "loose bees," "the poor man" and "the poor dog" Then the plea for him to come in a hurry.

It didn't make sense. Allison had been cultivating honey for as long as he could remember, and if she'd ever had a problem with her bees, he didn't recall it. Besides, Danny and Romeo were both too smart and too tough to be taken down by a few bees.

It wasn't until he was out of the truck and standing face-to-face with hands-down the most perfect specimen of womanhood to ever float down from heaven, that it began to make a scary kind of sense. The fact that Ms. Perfection was also crazy was the piece of the puzzle that made all the others slip into place.

Instinctively his heart went back to jackhammering in his chest.

"Where's my dog?" he demanded.

"Doc Allison is inside with him. Please, you have to listen," she said, stepping directly into his path and raising both palms. As if that could stop him—or save her—if he felt like doing something more than listen. "I can't tell you how sorry…"

That was enough to confirm his suspicion that whatever the nature of the crisis, she was to blame. Not exactly a surprise.

"Get out of my way," he ordered, prepared to move her physically if she made it necessary.

She stepped aside, proving she had at least a modicum of sense.

He strode through the deserted waiting area and headed for the examining room. First he would check on Romeo. Then he would deal with the lunatic outside.

He shoved open the door without taking time to knock.

Romeo, all 140 pounds of him, was lying on his side on the examining table. A narrow white cloth covered his eyes, and the rest of him was covered with swollen bumps, some of then with gauze stuck to them. Bee-stings. Dozens of them, damn her. The six-year-old German shepherd was absolutely motionless. Doc sat on a stool by his side, her head in her hands. Gretchen was in the corner, looking even gloomier than usual.

At the sound of the door opening, the vet's head jerked up.

"Damn, Doc," he blurted before she had a chance to speak. "He's not…"

He couldn't even say it.

"No, no. Of course, he's not," Doc Allison assured him as she quickly stood and rounded the examining table to give his arm a comforting squeeze. "I have him sedated. Once the painkillers and antihistamines do their thing, he should be as—" she caught herself and shrugged "—make that not quite as good as new, not right away at least, but we can make him reasonably comfortable. It's Dan I'm really worried about. Did you know he was allergic to beestings?"

Owen shook his head. "He is?"

"Severely so, judging by the difficulty he was having breathing." Her lips tightened as she added, "Of course, a hundred or so beestings would overwhelm just about anyone's nervous system."

The mental image made him grimace. "What the hell happened?"

She shook her head and plunged her hands deep into the pockets of her wet, rumpled lab coat.

For the first time he noticed that she was wet all over. Her hair was hanging in damp clumps, and her makeup was streaked across her face.

"You look awful, Doc."

"Thanks. I feel even worse." She dragged her hair back from her forehead. "As for what happened…I'm not exactly sure myself. Oh, I have a grasp of the highlights, but the details are sketchy, and to tell you the truth, I'm a little afraid that if I don't get a handle on my temper before I try to get details, I might end up behind bars before this day is over."

"Would the charge be justifiable homicide?"

"You tell me. I found out only a few minutes ago that you're the guy who had the coffee dumped on him."

"True."

"Why?"

"Long story. Comes down to her not liking to have her butt squeezed without her permission. Now let me hear the highlights about this afternoon."

She turned to Gretchen.

"Keep an eye on him, will you?" she asked with a nod toward Romeo. "Let me know when he starts to come around."

She motioned for Owen to follow her to her office. "Come sit down and I'll tell you what I know. If I'm in luck—which would be close to a miracle considering how it's been running lately—there might be a couple of cold beers hiding in the back of the fridge. My guess is I'm not the only one who could use one about now."

In the outer office Olivia was pacing and rehearsing her apology. When it came to apologies, she wasn't what you'd call a seasoned veteran. Oh, she'd uttered her share of *sorry*s for bumping into someone or not returning a phone call or breaking curfew when she was younger, but this was different. Her brow puckered as she tried to recall ever making a seriously heartfelt apology to anyone, for anything. She couldn't.

Not that she never made mistakes. Not by a long shot. But when she did mess up or fail to do something, there was always someone to step in and handle it. There were never any unpleasant consequences. Not for her anyway.

The realization bothered her. It was bad enough that she had been buffered her entire life from the consequences of her own actions, but to be so utterly oblivious, so completely self-focused that she never gave the matter a second thought, was not something to be proud of.

Perhaps if she had taken the heat on occasion, she wouldn't be fumbling for the appropriate words now that she needed them. This was a major-league screwup and it required a major-league apology. Even if she came up with one that was letter perfect, and even if Rancourt and her boss remained calm long enough to accept it, there was no hope of saving her job. She had only slightly more experience with work practices than with apologies, but it was enough to know her days at Danby Animal Hospital were history.

She wouldn't think about that now.

Instead she looked around to see what else she could do to demonstrate how truly sorry she was. So far she had swept up the mess outside, rescheduled the few patients who hadn't fled and searched—unsuccessfully—for the real culprit in all this, Izzy, the feline Houdini with the disappearing act.

While she could happily strangle the cat, part of her longed for the sound of his bandaged paw tapping on the door for someone to let him in. Not for his sake. For hers. Losing a patient only added to the body count. It would also squelch any slight chance she might have of Doc Allison giving her, if not a favorable recommendation, at least not a warning for potential employers to run for their lives.

She couldn't think about that now, either.

Who was she kidding? She had to think about it and fast. If she didn't find another job immediately, she would be heading home with a white flag flying from the antenna of her dilapidated car. She shuddered, then stiffened her backbone. That was not going to happen, she promised herself. She would do anything, *anything*, to win this bet.

She drummed her fingertips on the desk, brooding about how much less humiliating this would be if one of the offended parties hadn't turned out to be the man from the diner. She'd toyed briefly with taking the stance that this somehow evened the score between them. Very briefly. Having your fanny patted seemed benign compared to being hauled away in an ambulance.

If only she'd had enough self-control to stop herself from dumping coffee on him, everything would be different. She might still be wearing her ruffled apron. And her father's frequent reminder that "What goes around comes around" wouldn't be ringing in her head loudly enough to bring on a migraine. But she didn't have that much self-control, and the prospect of apologizing while trapped in the glare of Rancourt's steel-and-ice gaze made her wish she knew where Izzy was hiding so she could join him.

She wondered how Rancourt would react once he heard her out. Not by shouting or lashing out, not if the tightly leashed control she'd witnessed last time was any indication. Not knowing what she was up against added to her anxiety. She dealt with it by rearranging the objects on the desk, all the time listening for footsteps so she wouldn't be taken off guard. She was willing to say she was sorry because it was the honest truth, but she wasn't willing to have anyone think she was nervous enough to jump out of her skin. Even if that was true, too.

After what seemed hours, Doc Allison walked in followed by Owen Rancourt. The instant he walked into the room, his gaze found Olivia and settled on her. And from that same instant, an edgy awareness of the man tingled inside her. As if that weren't distraction enough, Olivia had a sense of the air around her becoming heavy, as if a storm were brewing.

She got to her feet, cleared her throat and tried to keep her eyes on her boss. It wasn't easy with Rancourt's unwavering gaze drawing hers back to him.

"How is he? Romeo, I mean?" she asked.

"Resting," the vet replied, her tone clipped. "Has the hospital called with any word about Danny?"

Olivia shook her head. "I could call over there and—" Eager to please, she was already reaching for the phone when Doc Allison's voice cracked like a whip.

"No."

"I was just going to call and see if there is—"

"No." Her tone was razor edged. "Don't call. Don't check. Just don't do or touch anything. Do you understand?"

Olivia nodded.

"I understand you two have already met," the vet continued.

"Not formally," said Rancourt.

Doc Allison made it formal.

Olivia cleared her throat. "I'm glad I have this chance to talk to both of you together. I want to apologize…to both of you." Her voice held steady in spite of the fact that every word she'd prepared had slipped away like water down a drain. "Everything that happened today was entirely my fault. I didn't mean for it to happen. I was trying to do the best job I could, but somehow… First the cat wanted to use the litter box…at least that's what he wanted me to believe, when in reality he was planning to escape all along. I chased him, which was probably my second mistake…''

The expressions on their faces made her feel as if she had suddenly lapsed into Swahili.

"Where was I?" she asked. "Oh, right, the chase. I'm in pretty good shape, but this cat was faster, much faster, even with a bandaged paw. The next thing I knew I was on the other side of the bushes…and then the snake…and the bees." The halfhearted toss of her hands reflected her feeling of being overwhelmed by it all. "I tried. I really did, but everything I did wrong just led to something even worse."

She paused, waiting for one of them to speak. Somewhere, way in the back of her head, she could hear her mother's comforting voice saying to her the words she so often had, *You tried, sweetheart, that's what matters.*

"Say something," she urged.

"All right," obliged Doc Allison. "You're fired."

Obviously the woman did not share her mother's philosophy when it came to mistakes.

"I guess I deserve that."

"You guess?"

"I meant I do deserve it." She knotted her hands at her waist, dropped them back to her sides, finally folding them across her chest. "And I'm sorry. That might sound feeble or perfunctory, but I don't know what else to say. I wish I could go back and undo everything that happened today, but I can't. I can try to make it up to…"

"No," the other woman blurted.

"I was going to say make it up to Danny. Maybe take care of his hospital bills…and Romeo's, too, for that matter. I'd really like to take care of everything…and I mean *everything*."

Rancourt finally spoke, his eyes narrowed with suspicion . "You're willing to pay the bills?"

"Yes. I am."

"And just where does someone who's lost two jobs in less than a week come up with that kind of money?"

"I'll figure out something," she assured him.

Actually she already had it all worked out in her head. More than likely the bills wouldn't have to be paid for weeks. By that time she would have won the bet and she'd be back home, with full access to her checking account...and her credit cards and a car that didn't refuse to start three times out of five and her own beautiful bathroom, with its plentiful hot water and soft, thick towels, which she'd never appreciated until she was forced to share a bath with strangers in a rooming house.

She stopped herself before she broke down and wept, and refocused in time to hear Rancourt's response.

"That's not good enough."

Her jaw lifted and her brows arched before the words *Who the hell does he think he is?* had finished forming in her head. Somehow she managed not to give voice to the question.

"That's unfortunate," she replied. "I've apologized, lost my job and offered to handle whatever expenses are incurred. I really don't know what more I can do to rectify the situation."

"I do," he said.

She didn't trust the sudden gleam in his eyes and she didn't have time to figure out exactly why. One downward sweep of those thick, dark lashes and his gaze was once again as unreadable as smoke. How did a man become so skilled at blanking out? And why?

"I'm listening," she told him. "Tell me what more I can do."

"It's obvious. You need a job. I need someone to fill in for Dan until he's out of the hospital. Doc says he shouldn't be laid up too long, and she's agreed to hold off firing you, provided you agree to our plan."

"I don't understand where you're going with this," she said, afraid she knew exactly where he was going, hoping she was wrong. "Are you suggesting I work for you?"

"I'm not suggesting anything. I'm stating facts. You've been fired from two jobs in a matter of days. In case you're a hopeless optimist, let me assure you that folks around here won't be lining up to hire you. Do it my way and you'll give things time to settle down. And if you follow orders and don't maim me or burn the place down, when Dan's back on his feet, I'll help you line up something else and put in a good word for you."

"Why?"

"I guess I've got a thing for crazy ladies. Besides, I need someone right away. You're a risk I ordinarily wouldn't let within fifty yards of my place, but all things considered, I figure you've got more incentive than anyone to work hard and get it right." One broad shoulder lifted carelessly. "Then there's the little fact that you owe me. Double."

Payback time…just as she suspected.

"Are you in?" he asked.

"Not so fast. If by owing you double you're referring to the coffee incident, you deserved every last drop. We're even on that score. As for today, I've admitted I'm responsible and…" She hesitated, desperately wishing she had an option that didn't involve Owen Rancourt or wearing a turban until her hair grew back. She didn't. And they both knew it.

She sighed. "When do I start?"

He almost smiled. "No time like the present."

Chapter Four

When Rancourt explained that he expected her to *live* at his place as well as work there, Olivia's response had been quick and succinct.

"In your dreams," she told him.

She expected him to parry. Instead, in that irritatingly placid way he had, he informed her that he never dreamed, he wasn't offering her a nine-to-five job, and she wasn't the one giving the orders. His subtle emphasis on the last part ruffled her pride and she dug in her heels. It appeared they were at an impasse until Doc Allison intervened.

The vet attributed Olivia's opposition to concern for her own safety. Belatedly it occurred to Olivia that it probably should be. Moving in with a man she barely knew, and who had reason to dislike her, qualified as one of the risks she had given her word not to take.

The other woman went on to say she understood her

wariness and applauded it. She then offered her personal assurance, based on years of friendship, that Owen Rancourt was a man of honor and completely trustworthy.

Olivia wasn't buying the honorable part. She also held that trusting a man enough to be his friend was one thing; trusting him enough to be alone with him, in an isolated camp located in the middle of the heavily wooded no-man's-land between Danby and the rolling foothills several miles north, was quite another. None of which changed the fact that she needed the damn job. And now that she thought about it, free accommodations would be a bonus.

If he proved to be less honorable than Doc Allison claimed, well, she was able and willing to do whatever necessary to halt unwanted overtures...as Mr. Owen Rancourt well knew.

As she vacillated, the vet went on to explain that in addition to the main house, there were a number of cabins on the property, where handlers bunked when training camp was in session. The news that she wouldn't actually be living under the same roof with Rancourt tipped the scales and Olivia grudgingly agreed to give the arrangement a shot.

"Don't worry, you'll be perfectly safe with Owen," Doc Allison reassured her. "I wouldn't lie to another woman about something like that."

"Not even me?" she challenged, feeling as close to sheepish as she ever got. "The woman who threw this place into chaos in only two days?"

"Actually it was closer to one and a half," the vet corrected. "And no, not even you. I *like* you, Olivia. You're bright and funny. I just don't think you were the right person for me."

"And you think I am the right person for him?" Olivia gestured toward Rancourt.

Doc Allison's forehead furrowed and she sputtered a bit before saying, "To be honest, Olivia, I'm not sure who you would be right for. But Owen is in a bind and he's willing to take you on, so all I can say is…good luck to both of you."

She urged them toward the door with an unmistakable air of relief. "I could have told you there was nothing to worry about," Rancourt informed her when they were alone outside. "You'll be working so hard all day, and so worn-out every night, you won't have the time or energy to get yourself in trouble with me."

"It's not me I was worried about," she retorted.

His silence left her guessing whether his comment had been intended to put her at ease, or tick her off. She had no patience for guessing games when she was the one doing the guessing. Fortunately, her dealings with men seldom involved guesswork. Among close friends, she boasted a nearly flawless track record for assessing and categorizing a man, any man, within minutes of meeting him. That was one more reason it annoyed her that this particular man refused to stay where she put him.

He succeeded in shifting her impression of him yet again by opening her car door for her. It wasn't only that he did it; it was the *way* he did it…smoothly, effortlessly, as if the gesture were ingrained, rather than performed to impress. It wasn't what she expected from a man who would paw a woman he'd never met to amuse his buddies.

To her chagrin, he insisted on accompanying her to the house where she was staying and waiting outside while she packed and settled her bill. That accom-

plished, she followed him the twelve miles from town
to the road that accessed his land. A sign reading Canine
Training Camp marked the private road in white block
letters on a black background. No logo, no wasted
words. Pretty much like the man himself, she mused.

The road they turned onto was paved but narrow, so
narrow in places that tree branches scraped and slapped
her car windows. Since it was late October, most of the
leaves had already fallen, blanketing the ground with a
patchwork of fiery red and gold. Here and there a tree
clung defiantly to its last few leaves, refusing to surrender to nature.

Olivia was on the side of the rebel trees, even if theirs
was a losing battle. How long could a solitary tree hold
out against a force so much stronger and more relentless? A rueful smile curved her lips as she contemplated
the man at the wheel of the truck hurtling down the
road ahead of her and acknowledged an even more por-
tentous question: How long could she?

"Six weeks…max," she muttered to herself. Surely
Dan what's-his-name would recover and be back at
work sooner than that. Maybe a lot sooner. *Please give
me the—* She frowned. *Give me whatever it takes to put
up with Owen Rancourt for as long as I have to.*

A white house came into view on her right. The main
house, she decided. Olivia wasn't sure what she had
expected, a log cabin maybe, or a crumbling old farm-
house. Definitely not this. For one thing, the sprawling
one level home wasn't that old. It also wasn't crumbling. Not even close. With its brick front, glossy black
trim and freshly mowed lawn, it appeared fresh and well
tended. A front porch with several wooden rockers at
one end added a welcoming, almost old-fashioned touch
that an architect might decree was at odds with the style

of the house itself, but somehow it worked. But then, why should Rancourt's home be any easier to pigeon-hole than he was?

The house was situated on a small rise. She parked where he indicated, and as she got out of the car, she was able to make out the shapes of a group of smaller structures a short distance away. What she didn't see in the fading light was what she feared most, marauding packs of dogs. Maybe her luck was changing. Rancourt had said he needed help *getting ready* for the next train-ing session. Maybe there wouldn't be any dogs around till then. Except Romeo, that is.

A slight shudder rippled through her as she recalled her up-close-and-personal view of his teeth earlier. Then she remembered what followed and groaned inwardly. Was it possible for a dog to bear a grudge, she fretted? Maybe she would never have to find out. If her luck truly was changing, perhaps Romeo wouldn't be feeling up to coming home until she'd done her time and was out of there. A sudden bark, echoed by another and another put a quick end to her delusions of changing fortune.

She glanced around to pinpoint the direction of the barking and caught Rancourt watching her. The know-ing arch of her brows did not deter him. He wasn't smiling or frowning, but it would be a mistake to de-scribe his expression as vacant. On the contrary, he ap-peared alert and interested, intensely so. Owen Rancourt made no secret that he was thinking, she realized, only of what he was thinking about.

The barking persisted.

"Dogs," she said simply. Idiotically.

"What were you expecting?"

She shrugged. "Dogs."

"Good. I'd have hated to disappoint you right out of the gate."

He turned, lowered the rear of the truck and grabbed a thick coil of cable. Looping it over his shoulder, he reached for another. Next he rummaged through a box of what looked to Olivia like metal clamps and similar junk. Guy stuff, and slightly below dust on the list of things she found interesting. The rear view of the guy himself was a different matter.

It was with considerable interest that she took advantage of his preoccupation to check him out. Her gaze roamed over his broad shoulders and long legs. She liked the way his faded jeans rode low on his hips. As much as she would prefer to disdain every last thing about the man, she was forced to admit he had a nice butt. And great thighs. But then, Neanderthals often did. It was somehow linked to the excess of testosterone pumping through their veins, and other places. A private theory, but one she fully expected science to someday confirm. As a rule she wasn't much attracted to Neanderthals. But for some reason, tonight she was…

Losing it. She must be if she was secretly ogling Rancourt and enjoying it. It was simply because she'd been away from civilization too long, she assured herself, turning away and shifting her attention to the shadowy terrain below. It was nowhere near as captivating a sight, and she felt suddenly restless. What she wouldn't give for a glass of chilled chardonnay. And a cigarette. Which was telling, since her last smoke had been in the girl's lav her junior year at Covington Prep.

Behind her, the sounds of clinking metal persisted. She was about to tell him to hurry it up. Her feet hurt. If she'd known when she was dressing that morning that she would be chasing a renegade cat through bushes, she would have worn boots with a low heel. She hoped Izzy had turned up safe and sound. Not wanting to dwell on the other possibility, she wiggled her toes and heaved an impatient sigh that evolved into a yawn.

Not only did her feet hurt; she was exhausted. And grimy. She closed her eyes and could almost feel herself sliding into a deep tub of hot water, almost smell the fragrance of the soapy bubbles caressing her from shoulders to toes. She couldn't wait to get to her cabin and collapse.

The slamming of the truck's tailgate made her jump.

She turned to tell him it was about time, but his nasty expression stopped her.

"Don't worry about lending a hand," Rancourt said, biting out the words. "It took a while, but I've got it all under control now."

The sight of him weighted down with cables, more bulky stuff clamped under both arms, made her even more glad she'd bitten her tongue.

"Sorry," she said. "Do you want me to take something?"

She reached out. He took a step back.

"No. It's been a long day and I'd rather just leave well enough alone."

"I probably should at least carry my own bag."

"You definitely should carry your own bag," he retorted. "But you can get it later, when I show you your cabin…and when I'm not standing around holding an extra hundred pounds."

"Sorry," she said again. "I guess I just got lost in…the view."

She gestured in the direction of the foothills in the distance.

"Figures. It's really something, isn't it?"

Olivia turned to take another look, just to make sure he wasn't still being sarcastic. He couldn't possibly be. The rolling silhouette of the foothills, backlit by the sun setting in an ink-blue sky, was truly mesmerizing.

"My God, it is beautiful," she said softly. "It almost takes my breath away."

"Yeah. Mine, too. Night after night."

The barking had stopped, now it started up again.

"Let's move it. Sounds like the welcoming committee is getting restless." There was brusque affection in his tone now. Even his impossibly square jaw seemed to have softened slightly.

"Are they tied up?" she inquired, endeavoring to sound merely curious, rather than hair-trigger nervous. If she ever decided to take on the responsibility of being a pet owner, she would choose one of those fluffy little dogs you could carry around in your purse. If the barking was any indication, the members of the "welcoming committee" were neither fluffy nor little.

"Tied? You mean chained?" He sounded offended. "My dogs are never chained."

Her stomach seesawed. "Never?"

"No need. If you've got control of a dog, a word or a hand signal is as good as a chain."

"And if you don't have control?"

"Then you're a damn fool. I wouldn't keep a dog around I couldn't control with my voice alone."

"What would you do with him?"

"Shoot him," he said matter-of-factly, and started walking toward the house.

Olivia hurried to catch up. "Shoot him? You mean with a gun?"

He slowed enough to eye her dubiously. "Yeah, Olivia, I mean with a gun."

"Isn't that rather drastic?" she asked, falling into step with him again.

"No. It's smart."

"But what if that particular dog just didn't click with you? As an individual, I mean. Maybe another—"

"'Click'?" He sounded appalled. "I'm not running a dating service, for God's sake. I'm turning dogs into lethal weapons. And I'm the best there is at doing it. If I can't bring a dog to heel, that's a dog the world is better off without."

They walked a few yards before she said, "What makes you think you're the best?"

"I don't think it. I know it." He slanted her a self-satisfied smile and cocked his head toward the barking, which sounded louder and nearer with each step they took. "Of course, if you want a second opinion, you can ask them."

"Why are they barking that way?"

"They're glad I'm home. And they're hungry. They heard my truck and they want to know what's taking me so long. Then, too, they might've picked up on you."

"Me? Why me?"

"A woman's voice is pretty much a novelty around here."

"I see. I guess that means you're not married." Another dumb remark. But not, she realized, as dumb as not even considering the possibility he might be married until that moment. There was just something about him, that classic lone wolf demeanor of his, that said—no, screamed—that he was a man who made his way through the world alone and liked it that way.

"No, I'm not married," Rancourt replied with a faint, knowing smile. "Thanks for being interested."

The man had a real talent for being irksome.

"Trust me, I'm not. I was making conversation."

"Okay. Let's make conversation. You shouldn't have needed to ask if I was married."

"How?"

"If I did, there'd be a light in that front window for me when I got home. And you wouldn't have needed Doc's word that you'd be safe here."

"Maybe. Maybe not."

He took the porch steps in one stride and started to set his load down a short distance from the front door, piece by piece.

"Care to explain?" he asked without looking up.

"It just seems to me that a man who'd put his hands on another woman when he has a wife at home, could be capable of other indiscretions, as well."

"Makes sense." He straightened and met her gaze. "Hypothetically at least, since I don't have a wife."

"Right. Hypothetically."

"Come on," he said, pulling open the door. "I'll introduce you to the family I do have."

He reached inside to turn on the light.

Olivia hesitated. "Maybe you should go in first."

"You can tell your teeth to stop chattering," he advised, humor lurking in his deep voice. "They're in the yard out back. It's fenced."

"How is a fence any different from a chain?"

"A fence is a necessity when I have to leave them here alone. They still have plenty of freedom to move around, choose whether they want to be in the shade or sun, run, sleep."

"And a chain?"

His expression took on a note of contempt. "There are no good options with a chain. And listing the drawbacks would take too long. It amounts to this—a long chain risks a dog getting tangled around something and hurting himself trying to get free. A short chain will eventually break his spirit.''

''I see.'' It was good that she lacked the energy to challenge his opinion, because she couldn't find anything in it to disagree with. She had to settle for a disgruntled ''And my teeth were not chattering'' as she stepped past him on her way inside.

The interior was as much a surprise as the house itself. But it shouldn't be, she realized, after looking around. She'd heard somewhere that a perfectly decorated home reflects the unique personality of those who live there. If that was so, this place qualified for Decorator's Dream Home of the Year.

If she'd been asked to conjure up a decorating scheme to convey Rancourt's personality, this would be it. No frills, no extras, no nonsense. Apparently the man was no more enamored of excess ''stuff'' than he was unnecessary words. She might not be able to literally count the pieces of furniture he owned on the fingers of one hand, but that was the impression. Add that to the bare wood floors, windows clad only in white wooden blinds and the total absence of *tchotchkes* and you could sum up in a single word, austere.

''What's the verdict?'' he asked.

''I beg your pardon?''

He'd shut the door and was leaning against it. ''You were looking around as if you're thinking of buying the place. I'm curious what you think of it?''

''The truth?''

''Nothing but.''

Olivia shrugged. ''You asked for it. I think a monk's cell would have more charm.'' Taking a peek around the corner into the white and stainless steel kitchen, she added, "More pizzazz too, for that matter."

Rancourt nodded with satisfaction. "That's exactly the look I was going for, boring and monkish. You might as well get it straight right now—charm and pizzazz aren't on my list of priorities."

"How about comfort? What kind of man puts only one comfortable…" She strolled across the room to press her palm to a seat cushion. "Make that one semi-comfortable chair in front of the TV? And a thirteen-inch TV, at that."

"A man who doesn't entertain much…or watch much TV. Which, for the record, is a nineteen-inch."

She glanced from him to the TV and back. "But there's no DVD player, not even a VCR and not a single remote in sight. An American male without a remote suggests gender issues, if you ask me."

"Then I'll be sure not to. Come on out back and I'll introduce you."

It wasn't fair, Olivia groused silently, that he should be so impervious to her baiting when almost everything about him irritated her. It wasn't until they reached the screened porch, which opened off the kitchen, igniting an even more spirited round of barking, that she remembered to be scared.

"Maybe you should feed them first," she suggested. "I know how much I hate socializing on an empty stomach."

"No." He turned on a small table lamp and unlatched the porch door, then glanced over his shoulder at her before opening it. "You're not afraid, are you?"

She badly wanted to scoff at the very notion, but something about the size of the shadows circling on the other side of the thin screening compelled her to tell the truth. "As a matter of fact, I am," she confessed. "Very afraid."

"Good. You don't need to be, but it would be foolish for you to assume that on your own."

He opened the door and stepped outside. Instantly the dogs were all over him, leaping up and yipping for his attention, which he managed to dole out equally. At first she was unable to tell how many there were. A dozen, it seemed. As they settled down she was surprised to count only three dogs, two as big as Romeo and one even bigger.

He shoved the door wide with his shoulder and invited her to join them.

She hesitated. "You're really sure you can control them?"

With an indignant glance her way, he issued a single curt order to sit, and the dogs lined up before him like seasoned soldiers.

Olivia stepped just outside, but no further. Even if he could control them, she wasn't taking any chances.

"The big guy here is Radar, because that's what he's like when he's on a scent," he explained, reaching down to scratch around the ears of the largest of the three—a massive dog with a sleek, brown coat and woebegone expression. "He's 100 percent bloodhound, from the breed's premiere bloodline." In a clipped, slightly louder tone, he ordered, "Radar, make nice."

The dog got to his feet and approached Olivia, who promptly stiffened and hid her hands behind her back.

"Olivia, make nice," he drawled, his tone dry. "He only wants to smell your hand."

Cautiously she stretched out one hand. Radar's wet nose and tongue made contact simultaneously. She gave a little gasp of surprise, but managed to hold her hand steady. "I thought he only wanted to smell me."

"And maybe slobber over you a little bit," he added, shrugging when she took her eyes off the dog long enough to shoot him a withering look. He spoke the dog's name in that same clipped tone, and Radar's head came up, his velvet-brown eyes riveted on Rancourt, eager anticipation in his stance. Rancourt made a simple movement of his right hand, and the big dog returned to his place in line. A second hand movement had him stretched out on the floor, gazing up at his owner with the undivided attention she'd expect him to reserve for a raw T-bone steak.

"Good, Radar. Mac, make nice," he ordered.

This time she didn't have to be prodded to offer the tan-and-black dog the same hand she had just wiped dry on her slacks, and she flinched only slightly when she felt his rough tongue. "This breed I recognize," she said. "He's a German shepherd, right?"

"To the core," he confirmed. "Mac is short for Mac Cool, for obvious reasons. Mac's a real character."

She laughed. "He does have a certain roguish quality."

He called for the dog's attention and repeated the same hand motions to get him to retreat and lie down.

"And finally, in defiance of the 'ladies first' rule, since it's rank that matters most in the dog world, this is Jez, short for Jezebel." Bending to stroke the dog's side, he added, "Also, for obvious reasons, if you equate the name Jezebel with being cocky and shameless."

"Well then, Jezebel and I should hit it off just fine, because a lot of people I know have come to equate those same qualities with the name Olivia."

Rancourt regarded her speculatively. "Now what kind of woman brags about a thing like that?"

"The kind of woman who chooses to take it as a compliment, regardless of how it was intended."

Interest flared in his dark eyes. "Sounds like maybe I'm not the only one with gender issues." Without waiting for a response, he gave Jezebel the command to make nice.

Olivia, comfortable with the ritual by now, was relaxed enough to pet Jezebel in return. Like Mac Cool, she was a shepherd, but slightly smaller than the male and with a much prettier face. Olivia said so out loud.

"You're very observant. That's actually part of the criteria used to evaluate the breed. A male shepherd is supposed to have a decidedly masculine look and a bitch has a look that's gentler, more feminine."

"No gender issues in the shepherd world, I take it?"

"None," he agreed, nearly smiling. "Makes mating a hell of a lot simpler."

She scoffed. "Where's the fun in that?"

Something deeper than curiosity gleamed in his eyes now. "Is that what you like in a mate, Olivia, a challenge?"

"Sure. I keep hoping I'll come across one I can't conquer without breaking a sweat."

"Is that a fact?"

"Nothing but." Her smile was intended to goad. "Shocked? If you're not too shy to say you're the best at what you do, why should I be?"

His sudden grin revealed a dimple in his left cheek and a hint of one in his right, neither of which she'd noticed before. From nowhere came the thought that he ought to smile more often.

"Sounds like you and Jez will get along just fine," he said.

"You mean now that my teeth have stopped chattering," she added, deadpan. "Joking aside, though, I have to admit I'm impressed with the way you handle them. What else can you make them do?"

"The usual," he told her. "Fetch, roll over, find human remains under a few feet of snow and mud in the middle of an ice storm."

Her brows shot up. "They can't really do that? Can they?"

Rancourt shook his head. "I was exaggerating. The truth is, only Radar and Mac can do it consistently. Jez isn't rated for cadaver searches. Yet."

"Very funny. Now I'm really impressed. I've heard of dogs tracking escaped prisoners and finding old people who'd wandered off alone, but it never occurred to me they could sniff out something so…" She was grasping for a delicate word for *dead.* "So subtle. And under such horrendous conditions."

"They do come in handy, considering folks don't only escape or wander off on nice spring days and soft terrain that's easy to scent. If they did, any dog could do search and rescue."

"Even a poodle?"

He shrugged. "Probably. All dogs have good noses. Only a few have the intelligence, a driving work ethic and the sheer ass-dragging tenacity to track even when they're tired and cold and wind shifts have got them running in circles."

Olivia watched his eyes as he spoke, heard the pride in his husky voice. "You weren't kidding when you referred to them as family. You really love them."

"Yeah, I really do." He opened the porch door and

waved her back inside. "Give me a minute to feed them and I'll show you where you'll be bunking."

First she noticed the smell.

As soon as Rancourt opened the door of the cabin where she would be staying, a cloud of damp, musty air engulfed them. All three dogs lifted their noses into the air, tails wagging.

"Look at them," Olivia said, her own nose wrinkling as she waved her hand in front of her face. "You'd think they liked that awful smell."

Shrugging, he reached inside for the light switch. "They like any smell."

"How open-minded of them," she muttered.

"If I'd had more notice, I'd have aired the place out for you. It's been closed up most of the summer and we had some pretty heavy rain right through August." He batted away a cobweb hanging across the doorway. "You can count yourself lucky that it's not too cold to sleep with a window open. Leave all the windows and the door open tomorrow and most of that musty smell will clear out."

By the time he finished speaking the fluorescent light overhead had flickered to life and shed enough harsh, white light for her to check out the inside of the cabin. Suddenly the smell of the place was no longer tops on the list of reasons she could not possibly stay there. It had been bumped down by the spider webs and peeling paint and that hideous easy chair upholstered in orange corduroy and dog hair.

Jez, Radar and Mac had made themselves welcome and were busy sticking their noses into every crack and crevice. Ordinarily she would have protested their tramping around the place she was expected to sleep, but really, what was the point?

"You have got to be kidding," she said.

He looked around, absently scrubbing his knuckles along his jaw. "The place needs a good cleaning, that's for sure. A fresh coat of paint wouldn't hurt, either."

"You're very optimistic," she retorted. "I was thinking more along the lines of using plastic explosives on it."

He chuckled and gave her a condescending pat on the back the way one of her brothers might have. "It's not as bad as it looks. Personally, I have complete confidence in your ability to whip this place back into shape in no time."

She felt her jaw drop. "You don't actually expect *me* to clean this cabin?"

"Actually, I expect you to clean this one plus the other seven. Starting first thing in the morning. We can talk about your afternoon chores over lunch."

Olivia laughed out loud. "You're mad. Even if I had any idea where to begin cleaning this place, I couldn't possibly do it in one morning…never mind seven others."

He lifted one broad shoulder. "You'll figure out something."

"What if I refuse?" she demanded, her chin in the air, hands planted on her hips.

"You mean what if you quit?"

The question put the brakes on her careening temper. She took a deep breath, thinking. She would like nothing better than to quit. It would be sheer heaven. And hell. Considering the likelihood of her finding another job within fifty miles of Danby, quitting was tantamount to surrendering. To Brad and to Rancourt.

If she hadn't been too tired to lift it, she would hit him over the head with her suitcase. She settled instead for a contemptuous glare. "What do you really want from me?"

"Only what our deal calls for. I expect from you what I'd expect from Danny, a full day's work for a full day's wages. How long that day lasts is up to you."

"My mistake," she retorted. "I thought I was taking the place of an employee, not an indentured servant."

"Get a good night's sleep, Olivia. Things will look better in the morning."

Owen signaled to the dogs and pulled the door shut on his way out.

As he walked away, he began counting. One. Two. Three. Fou—

Bang. Something he judged to be the approximate size of a woman's shoe slammed against the inside of the cabin door. It was quickly followed by something that sounded even heavier, and it didn't stop there. Grinning, he shoved his hands in his pockets and gave in to a sudden impulse to whistle. Somehow he had known she wasn't the type to sulk when she was angry. It may have taken a half second longer than he'd predicted for her to start tossing stuff, but once she had, she got a real nice rhythm going in no time.

It didn't bother him that she was tearing up one of his cabins. There was nothing close to delicate or valuable in any of them. Only an idiot—or someone without a clue about the ways of men and big dogs who'd rather be outdoors—would fancy up a place for them to bunk. Or think it would matter a bit to them either way. He wasn't an idiot. And he knew all about the habits of men and dogs whose passion involved trudging through thickets and swamps and anywhere else the scent led them.

Besides, she was the one who'd spend tomorrow cleaning up the mess she made tonight.

Even if none of that were true, however, he still wouldn't have stopped her. It was too damn satisfying to watch her rush headlong into a wall of frustration of her own making. It wasn't payback for the incident today or for her little tantrum in the diner, though it was obvious she thought it was. That would have been simple. This was complicated. There was something about Olivia that provoked and challenged and got under his skin in a way he didn't recognize. Maybe because the feeling she churned up inside him was one he'd never felt before. And maybe because she wasn't like any woman he'd ever met before.

For one thing she was more beautiful than any flesh-and-blood woman had a right to be. She was glossy, full-color, air-brushed, magazine-cover beautiful. Too perfect to be real. Too good to be true.

Complicating things even more was the fact that it wasn't passive beauty, the kind content to be worshiped from a distance. His whistling was interrupted by a quick grin. The man who made the mistake of worshiping Olivia would earn only her scorn for his trouble. And any man so tame he could be kept at a distance wouldn't get any part of her at all.

Olivia's beauty was hot and volatile and in-your-face. She didn't flaunt it. She didn't have to. It came off her in beams brilliant enough to make the air around her glow…and blur a man's vision and make him forget that something that seems too good to be true always is.

Just looking at her threatened to loosen inside him

something he knew could never be unleashed. That didn't stop him from hungering for her, or stop his head from filling with a jumble of confusing thoughts whenever he was near her—crazy thoughts of armored warriors and clashing swords, of conquering and claiming, of the ultimate triumph and the ultimate surrender known to man. Dangerous thoughts.

"You know what the trouble is, Mac?" The dog's ears went up as if he understood, which was comforting, since Romeo and the three dogs loping alongside were all he had. "The trouble isn't that she's too beautiful or too good to be true. The trouble is she's here."

It had been a mistake to bring her here. He'd known that even before he'd suggested it. But knowing it was a mistake hadn't stopped him from making it.

Now she was here. Right where he wanted her. Right where he'd been imagining her every night for more than a week. Well, maybe not exactly where he'd been imagining her, he acknowledged, recalling the heat of those fervent, late-night fantasies. But she was close. Closer than was safe, for either of them.

Could he handle it?

He would have to.

At his front door he paused for one last look back at the cabin where she would be sleeping. The light was still on. Was she still throwing stuff, he wondered? Or had she settled down to plot her revenge?

Chapter Five

She was going to find the most horrendous-smelling cheese known to man and hide a nice, ripe chunk of it in his car, in a spot it wouldn't be easily found.

She was going to send a Strip-o-Gram to him in the middle of Sunday dinner with his fiancée and her parents.

She was going to tell *their* parents how the summer he was twelve he'd bribed her to push him off the gazebo roof to get out of ballroom dance lessons at Miss Primrose's Academy.

Each time Olivia rinsed her sponge in the bucket of water, wrung it out and slapped it back onto the cabin floor, she added another item to the list of ways she was going to make her brother suffer. She'd run out of inventive and clever ideas a while ago and was now working her way through the obnoxiously childish. She was not ashamed.

He had it coming. If not for Brad, she wouldn't be stuck here in doggy-land and she definitely would not be on her hands and knees, scraping who-knows-what off the floor with a putty knife. Only a few hours ago she'd had but a vague notion of what a putty knife was, and would have preferred to keep it that way. Instead, thanks to dear Brad, she was wet and messy and very close to saying to hell with the other seven cabins and calling it a day.

The learn-as-you-go method of cleaning was exhausting. She refused to ask for help and risk revealing that she had never so much as made a bed from scratch in her life. Ordinarily she was not embarrassed by the truth. But ordinarily she didn't have to face the smug amusement such an admission was sure to draw from Owen Rancourt.

Mistakes were time consuming. Only after trapping herself in a corner did it occur to her one should always scrub a floor toward the door and not the other way around. When the final strip of blue vinyl floor was as clean as she could get it, she ditched the sponge and got to her feet, wincing at the sight of her waterlogged hands and two more broken nails. The one small consolation was knowing she would have a clean, fresh-smelling place to sleep in that night.

After dumping the dirty water, she stood and surveyed the results of her labor. The windows sparkled, the dirty handprints and paw prints were gone from the walls, and the sheets on the single bed had the sweet smell of being dried outdoors. She'd even draped a Hermes scarf over the bedside table to add a bit of panache. It was a cozy little hovel, if she did say so herself, and if she caught so much as a whiff of criticism from Ran-

court, she was going to have to do bodily injury…guard
dogs or no guard dogs.

Who knows? The dogs might even turn a blind eye
if she limited herself to breaking something small over
his head. Like, say, a ladder. Ever since she and the
Three Musketeers had bonded over a fried egg sandwich earlier that morning, they'd been casting eager
looks her way whenever they were in sight. Mac had
even pranced into the cabin as she was scrubbing the
floor and slid his nose under her arm so he could lick
her face.

Of course, the dogs had no way of knowing that if
she had it to do over, she wouldn't be so quick to part
with that sandwich. Rancourt had woken her far too
early by tossing a foil wrapped package on her bed. He
announced that she'd slept through the 6 a.m. breakfast
seating and that it was due solely to the kindness of his
heart that she was getting anything at all to eat.

She'd been stretched out on the bed fully clothed, her
boots still on. She hadn't wanted to so much as walk
barefoot in the place in the condition it was in. Half
asleep and cranky, she'd sat up, peeled back the foil
and proceeded to express her gratitude by feeding the
soggy sandwich to the dogs. That was hours ago. Since
then her attitude toward fried eggs had evolved almost
as much as her attitude toward cleaning.

She checked her watch and heaved a dejected sigh.
Two hours and seven dirty cabins until lunch. Assuming
she didn't collapse from hunger, there was no way she
would get to all of them this morning. Even her super-
cilious boss should realize that. Her teeth snapped together so suddenly she bit her tongue and cursed. How
gullible could she be? Of course he knew it, the rat.
This was a setup, a sneaky little game to humiliate her,

payback for the coffee incident. He'd arranged it so she would have to fail.

By her code, that meant failure was no longer an option. Resentment sizzled through her, kicking her energy level into overdrive.

Okay, Rancourt, you want war, you've got it.

She yanked her ponytail tighter and stripped off her sweater. It would be easier and faster to work in only her black tank top and jeans. She would clean his damn cabins so they were fit for royalty, and she would get it done before noon. And then she would turn the tables on that underhanded slave driver. After all, take away his perplexing blend of intimidation and charm and he was no different from any other man. And he was about to learn that any man who toyed with her did so at his own risk.

She lost track of time. Tasks that, hours earlier, had been as unthinkable as flying coach class she came to perform with near robotic efficiency. She swept and polished, sweated and muttered under her breath. At 12:35 she was standing in front of the cabin next to hers, paintbrush in hand, sore in places that were never sore even after the most vigorous workout at the health club.

She squinted at the cabin door, spied a spot she had missed and slapped the paintbrush back and forth across it. Perfect, she decided, and rested the brush on the open can of paint. She reached back and pressed her hands against her back, arching and stretching side to side to loosen her aching muscles.

Twenty yards away, Owen saw her and checked his long stride. A smile tugged at his lips. It was past lunchtime, and he was hungry, but he would never be hungry enough to pass up the opportunity to watch Olivia. Her black jeans weren't quite as enticing as the short, tight uniform she was wearing the first time he'd seen her, but it was still the prettiest sight to ever grace his property. He understood how a man could become so entranced he would have to reach out and touch. It didn't make it right. It was just something he understood.

Mac sprinted ahead to reach her first and nuzzled her thigh. Olivia smiled and stroked his head. That was one lucky dog, thought Owen.

"Hey, Mac," she crooned, then glanced in his direction. He saw her eyes narrow with suspicion. "What are you smiling at?"

"Was I smiling?" Owen rubbed his mouth with the back of one hand and shrugged. "Must be because I'm hungry and it's lunchtime."

She gave a decisive shake of her head. "No. That wasn't an oh-goody-it's-lunchtime sort of smile."

"That's a relief. I do my best to suppress my 'oh goody' tendencies in public." He moved closer, Jez and Radar at his heels. "Come on in and have lunch."

"You go ahead, I want to finish up here first."

He glanced at the freshly painted white door. "It looks finished to me."

"Yes, but I still have a way to go before I clean my brush." She gestured toward the other cabins.

"You do realize I was joking about having you paint the cabins?"

"You mentioned painting the inside," she replied, "which I have no intention of doing even if you weren't joking. I decided on my own that the front doors were in dire need of help. You know what they say about first impressions."

"I've heard. I guess we're the exception to the rule."

"How so?" she asked, the slight tilt of her head quizzical.

"Do you really need to ask?"

"Apparently, I do."

"I meant that you didn't exactly make the best impression the first time we met, and damned if I don't like you, anyway."

She looked aghast. "*I* didn't make the best impression? What about you?"

"What about me?" He smiled for the pleasure of seeing her heat up. "The way I see it, I behaved with the utmost respect and restraint given the circumstances."

"In that case, you're not only crass, you're delusional."

He gave a negligent shrug. "I've never had any complaints from women in the past."

"Well, you should have. What makes you think it's all right to grab a woman's butt first and give her a chance to complain later?"

"I'm delusional, remember? What makes you so sure I grabbed yours?"

"I was there, remember?"

"So was I."

"You were there, all right, with your hand still in midair when I turned, as if you'd just pulled back so you wouldn't get caught in the act."

"Or as if I'd just knocked someone else's hand away?"

The brilliant blue of her eyes gradually deepened; it was like watching the surface of a lake when the sun drifts behind a cloud.

"Is that what happened?" she demanded.

"Do you really want to know?"

"Of course I want to know," she snapped.

"Even knowing that if that was the way it happened, you drenched the wrong man?"

"I can live with that if you can." She swept impatiently at a loose tendril of hair near her cheek. "You just better be telling me the truth."

"There's one way for you to be sure of that," he said, moving close to her. "Decide for yourself."

Without looking away from her wary expression, he motioned the dogs down with one hand and reached for her with the other, curling his fingers around the back of her neck.

"What are you doing?" she demanded as his fingertips moved lower to slowly trail along her spine.

Her muscles tensed, and there was a revealing breathiness to her voice, but she didn't push him away.

"I'm helping you get at the truth," he explained, making an effort to concentrate. It would be so much easier to stop thinking altogether and surrender to the languor spreading through him, making his own muscles feel heavy.

With the hand that was not tracing small, lazy circles in the small of her back, he tucked that loose lock of hair behind her ear.

"Your hair sparkles in the sunlight. Like there's silver mixed in with the gold. Did you know that?"

She shook her head. A deep breath lifted her chest so that by leaning forward just a little he made contact. They both swallowed hard, their gazes still locked, his curious, hers cautious.

She'd tilted her head back to look up at him, and their faces were so close Owen could feel her breath on his lips. It made him crazy. When he saw the tip of her tongue slide across the perfect white line of her teeth, he felt as if his insides were the string on a bow and a power far beyond his control was drawing it further and further back.

He wanted to kiss her.

He wanted her to stop him.

Stop him from making another mistake he couldn't afford.

He bent his head. Her lips parted, and he swore he could feel her jolt of surprise when he settled for sliding his cheek over hers and letting his lips play lightly with the soft skin close to her ear. She felt like silk. She smelled like woman.

Drawing a steadying breath, he did what he'd set out to do and slid his hand down the last few inches to caress her bottom. He took his time, because it felt so damn good to touch her. And because he wanted to be in control when he stepped back to face her.

When he did, the fiery gaze he was accustomed to was veiled with confusion. He wondered if she had any idea how clearly her eyes telegraphed her mood.

He managed a small, challenging smile that was not returned. "So what's the verdict, Olivia?"

"What was the charge?" That quickly she was back in control, the spirit back in her eyes, the edge back in her tone.

He laughed appreciatively. "Illegal use of hands. Am I guilty or innocent?"

"Innocent," she pronounced grudgingly. "And don't go thinking that stupid little demonstration you just gave had anything to do with my decision. Because it didn't."

"Oh, no? What did?"

She shrugged and flicked an invisible speck of lint from her shirt. "I'm not sure, really. Call it a gut feeling."

"Fair enough. And you don't have a problem with the truth?"

"Why should I?"

"No reason, I suppose. I just thought it might bother you to know that somewhere on the mean streets of Danby walks a man who pawed you and got away with it."

The wheels in her head turned quickly. It seemed less than a second before the familiar rebelliousness flared in her eyes.

"Looks like you've got some temper to work off," he observed, his confidence due to the fact that he'd made a point to stand between her and the paint. Picking up the brush, he handed it to her. "I'll just leave your lunch on the kitchen table."

By the time she'd painted the last door, cleaned up and checked to make sure she hadn't missed anything, it was late afternoon and Olivia wasn't certain which she craved more, food or sleep. She mulled it over in the shower, adjusting the flow so a hot, hard stream of water poured down on her aching muscles, which was nearly every muscle in her body.

She toweled off, dried her hair and slathered her body with lotion, all on autopilot. In that same mode she laid out clean clothes. She got as far as putting on her underwear before her body made the choice for her: she wanted sleep. She collapsed on the bed and closed her eyes. It was only as she was drifting into sleep that her control slipped and she confronted the question she'd avoided all afternoon—amazing how distracting hard work could be. Now that her body was relaxed, her mind was free to roam, and something inside her was demanding an answer: Why the hell hadn't Rancourt kissed her when he'd had the chance?

He'd wanted to, that much was obvious. She'd felt the tension in him and the pounding of his heart when he'd pressed against her. She knew what that meant because her own heart had been pounding just as hard. His touch had made her shiver and yearn. She had been floating, willing to let him set the pace, certain he was dragging it out to excite her, to heighten the anticipation for both of them.

Then he'd pulled away. It was as if the moment had been cut short with a machete, leaving her wanting and bewildered and resentful. Now she was only exhausted and resentful. She was going to have to do something about that. And him. As she rolled to her side and snuggled into the pillow, she issued herself a vague reminder to give the matter some more thought later.

She dreamed about him, and about a different ending for their little interlude. In her dream he didn't pull away from her. Instead he turned his head and his mouth touched hers, as gently as it had brushed against the side of her throat. When the gentleness disappeared and he deepened the kiss, she yielded to him and to the mysterious feeling swirling inside her. The feeling warmed and lulled her. His hands scorched every place they touched. He touched her everywhere. The dream dead-ended there, leaving her as confused and wanting as the real thing.

It didn't help when she opened her eyes and saw him standing beside the bed. Olivia blinked rapidly, expecting him to melt back into her subconscious. As usual, he refused to cooperate. Disoriented, she noted that the lamp on the nightstand had been turned on and Rancourt was wearing the same clothes as yesterday. Unless yesterday was really today.

"Did I miss breakfast again?" she asked him, a sleepy huskiness in her voice. She raised up on one elbow and swept her hair back from her face.

For several seconds he appeared mesmerized by the simple act and then seemed to remember she was waiting for an answer and cleared his throat. "Just once so far today, along with lunch and dinner. But from the sound of it you probably would have been out through breakfast tomorrow if I hadn't woken you."

"'The sound of it'?" she repeated.

"That's right. Don't worry, you're cute when you snore."

She sat up, suddenly wide awake. "I do *not* snore."

"Yeah, you do." He turned and reached with both hands for something on the chest of drawers behind him. "It's not the end of the world, especially since you may be the only woman in the world who even *snores* gorgeously. You're definitely the only woman I've ever seen pull it off. "

Olivia wasn't sure if that merited a thank-you or a pillow tossed at his head. She settled for grumbling, "I'm not surprised to hear that you make a habit of barging in on women uninvited and spying on them."

"At the risk of ruining the pleasure you derive from thinking the worst of me, I have to confess that you are the first woman I've ever barged in on uninvited. And this qualifies as a medical emergency."

She ran a disparaging gaze over him. "You look fine to me."

"I'm not the one who needs help." He glanced at the tray he was holding, then back at her. "I didn't want to have to explain why an indentured servant starved to death on my property.''

Immediately her attention shifted to the tray and the steaming plate of something that smelled wonderful.

"I hope you like beef Bourguignon better than fried eggs," he remarked.

"Beef Bourguignon? You're not serious?"

He lowered the tray so she could see—and smell—for herself.

"I adore beef Bourguignon," she told him, drinking in the aroma until her mouth watered.

"Good. Since the dogs have already eaten, I'm not sure what I would do with it if you turned your nose up. All set?"

"Yes." As she sat up straight, her gaze fell on her bare legs. "I mean no."

She was stretched out in bed wearing only cherry-red silk panties and a matching teddy. It wasn't as if he was seeing her naked, she hurriedly assured herself. Though he might well have, had she decided to take a nap *before* starting to dress and fallen asleep in what she usually wore to bed, which was nothing.

"I mean, I'm…"

He smiled appreciatively. "I noticed." He was still noticing and making no secret of it as he let his heated gaze stray over her. "It's not a problem."

"It will be if I spill something hot on myself and you have to rush me to the emergency room."

"It's a risk I'm willing to take," he assured her.

"I'm not. My robe is hanging in the bathroom. Would you mind getting it for me?"

"I mind like hell," he retorted, his rueful expression a different sort of flattery. "But I'll get it, anyway."

* * *

Wrapped in the white terry cloth robe, the tray on her lap, she took her first bite and closed her eyes to savor it. "It's delicious. Where did you get it?"

"Which part of it?"

She regarded him quizzically. "I beg your pardon?"

"I'm not sure what you're asking about. I got the carrots and mushrooms at the vegetable stand out by the high school. I already had the onions and the wine is from—"

"Very funny," she said. "Are you trying to tell me you made this?"

He nodded. "Surprised?"

"Stunned," she told him truthfully. "And very impressed."

"I'm glad you like it."

"I love it. It may even be the best I ever had. And I'm sort of an unofficial authority on the subject." The tray also held a glass of very fine merlot and crusty rolls with butter. And, most intriguing to her of all, a silver napkin ring with a genuine linen napkin. She took another bite, then a sip of wine.

"Where did you learn to cook like this?" she asked.

"The question isn't so much where as how. The answer is, out of desperation. My mother was a gourmet cook. Self-taught. That's one of her recipes."

"Where does the desperation come in?"

As she continued to eat, he stared into the darkness beyond the window, his mouth set in a brooding line. When she'd nearly cleaned her plate and given up on an answer, he finally spoke.

"She died when I was fourteen," he explained, still not looking at her. "My dad died a little while later. After that I was on my own."

"On your own at fourteen?" she exclaimed. "Wasn't there anyone who…"

"No." He shifted her gaze to meet hers. "And I don't talk about it."

Not, "I don't like to talk about it." Or, "I'd rather not talk about it." But "I don't talk about it." Period.

"I'm sorry. I wasn't trying to—"

"You didn't. I just don't talk about it. To anyone. Ever." The firmness of his tone made it clear the questions piling up in her head would have to remain there.

"I understand. And I see where the desperation comes in. If you live alone and you want to eat, you learn to cook."

"Actually, back then I ate a lot of canned stuff," he admitted. "As soon as I was old enough I enlisted in the marines. Six years of three square meals a day. Being selected for the K-9 unit was a bonus."

"Food and dogs, man's two best friends," she quipped. "What ever made you leave?"

"Nothing specific. I'd learned a lot and it got to a point where I wanted to train my dogs my way."

"Well, having seen the results, I'm amazed you had any time to learn to cook."

He smiled and shrugged. "Like I said, I was desperate. When it got so I couldn't drive past a fast-food joint without feeling queasy, I decided it was time to check out my mother's old recipe box."

"And a gourmet chef was born?" she teased, getting to her feet.

He took the tray from her. "Not even close. Let's just say there were a few meals I wouldn't even feed to my dogs."

"You've come a long way."

She picked up her comb and watched in the mirror

as he acknowledged the compliment with only a slight tip of his head.

"I've noticed you don't talk much," she remarked, frowning as her comb hit a snarl.

"I've noticed you do," he countered dryly.

"Thanks. I've been told it's part of my charm." Ignoring his snicker, she continued to comb her hair and watch him in the mirror. "Actually, I have four older brothers, all of them outspoken and assertive. Growing up, I had to hold my own or get lost in the shuffle."

"Four brothers, huh?" Amusement played at the corners of his mouth. "No sisters?"

"No sisters."

"That's a real shame," he drawled, his gaze darkening as it moved slowly from her face to her bare feet. For once she had no trouble reading his mind. Proof, if she'd needed it, that it was to her advantage to keep him on this track.

"I've always thought so, too," she said, sighing. "Just think of all the clothes I could borrow if I had four sisters instead of brothers."

"I was thinking of something else entirely."

The gaze that met his in the mirror said, "I know."

Out loud she said, "Oh, I can think of lots of advantages. For one thing, I wouldn't have had to agree to judge the boys' stupid peeing contests just so they would let me play with them."

She could see that caught him by surprise. Tossing aside the comb, she turned to face him before his raunchy grin finished forming. With her palm raised, she said, "Don't bother asking. I don't talk about it. To anyone. Ever."

They shared a laugh. Encouraged, Olivia folded her

arms across her chest, leaned back and rested the sole of one foot against the bathroom door frame.

"Okay, now that you know why I talk so much, how come you don't?"

He shrugged. "I guess I don't have much to say."

"Ah, a man of action, is that it?" she queried in a playful drawl.

She still couldn't figure out what had held him back earlier, but she had felt his heat and sensed the effort it cost him to let her go. Whatever his reason was, he was still in her cabin. The way he'd looked at her before consenting to get her robe, and the way even now his gaze kept drifting to the flash of bent leg revealed through the opening of her robe, all made her confident he couldn't pull it off twice.

"A man of action," he echoed, those heavy-lidded gray eyes giving away nothing. "I've never given it much thought."

"Maybe you should."

She said it off-handedly, as if she were offering to water his plants while he was on vacation. As if she weren't casually loosening the tie at her waist and letting her robe slip to the floor.

She moved toward him purposefully, watching him watch her. There was something revealing in his eyes now. Desire, pure and simple. She stopped close beside him and hesitated for a split second, allowing him to draw his own conclusions about what she was up to, before murmuring, "Excuse me," and reaching behind him for the sweater she'd left on the back of the chair earlier.

A muscle at the side of his jaw flexed, and when she reached behind him a second time, for her jeans, her breast pressing against his bicep, he caught his breath.

Once she gathered her clothes, Olivia took her sweet time putting them on, thinking of it as a reverse striptease.

There was no further reaction from Rancourt. Unless you counted the hint of amusement around his mouth as he tilted his chair onto its two back legs and hooked his hands behind his head to watch the show. She had selected the outfit with him in mind…though she hadn't anticipated he would be watching her dress. The jeans were her favorite, soft and faded and worn with a wide, black leather belt. They made the most of her long legs and willowy frame. And they made her red cashmere sweater seem even more vividly feminine than it already was, with its waist-skimming length and trio of small pearl buttons at the back of her neck. The fact that it coordinated so well with her lingerie was habit, signifying nothing.

Turning so her back was to him, she glanced over her shoulder and shot him a smile intended to dazzle.

"How about giving me a hand with these buttons, boss?"

"Boss?" he repeated, setting the chair right and getting up. "I suppose that's a step up from having you call me Rancourt in that snotty way of yours."

She decided to overlook that comment and silently lifted her hair so he could see what he was doing, surprised at the ease with which he fastened the tiny buttons. All too soon his warm hands fell away.

"That should do it," he told her.

She released her hair and shook it into place, twirling to face him before he had time to move away. Knowing the chair was at his back, she sidled as close to him as he had to her that afternoon. "You're pretty good with buttons."

"I try."

"I try, too, but I usually end up getting my hair caught or chipping a nail." The difference in height required her to tip her head back and look up at him. The subtle flutter of her long dark lashes she threw in voluntarily. "I wonder how I can thank you?"

"You just did."

"That's not enough. You have no idea how much I hate chipping my nails," she told him, her smile softening.

"I imagine it's high on the list," he returned with a droll expression. "I'll tell you what, next time I need help buttoning something, I'll call you."

"No you won't," she shot back. "You're too afraid of me."

He laughed, a brief, disparaging sound. "You can't seriously think I'm afraid of you."

"You're terrified."

"Careful, I think my delusions are rubbing off on you."

"It's not a delusion. It's a fact. Here's a couple more. When you had your arms around me outside today, you wanted badly to kiss me. You want to kiss me now. How about it, boss, truth or delusion?"

He didn't hesitate. "Truth. I did want to. I *do* want to."

"So do I," she said softly, smiling faintly as her hands slid up his chest and rested lightly on his broad shoulders.

He felt good, solid. Unexpectedly her hands trembled with excitement. She waited for his arms to leave his sides and wrap around her and was miffed when he failed to cooperate.

"You just missed your cue," she informed him, her

voice laced with impatience. "What kind of man doesn't recognize an invitation when it throws itself at him?"

He smiled indulgently. "A man who already has plans for tonight and is running late."

Chapter Six

Her hands were still pressed to his chest. Before Olivia could snatch them away, he covered them with his much bigger hands and held them there several seconds before letting her go. Neither the gesture nor the hint of regret in his tone as he gave her the brush-off, did anything to soothe her feelings of righteous indignation. She had a sudden urge to grab the tray and dump it over his head. He must have guessed as much, because he reached for it first and carried it with him to the door, out of her reach.

"You already have the key to this cabin," he said, pulling another from his pocket. "This is the key to the house. Feel free to watch TV and raid the refrigerator. There's a decent collection of books and music in one of the spare bedrooms, if you're interested."

She wasn't interested. She was furious, with him, with herself and with his *plans* for the night. Whoever she was, she was interfering with Olivia's agenda for the next six weeks. Six bloody weeks, that's all she needed. After that, anyone who wanted the man was welcome to him.

He shouldered the door open, saying. ''There's no reason you should be, but if you think you'll be uneasy here alone, I can leave one of the dogs with you, like Mac, since he seems to have the biggest crush on you.''

''That won't be necessary,'' she assured him coolly. ''And just for the record, the invitation I referred to entitled you to a friendly kiss, nothing more, and certainly not the rest of the night. It so happens I have plans of my own for tonight.''

''Then it worked out well,'' he countered, though clearly dubious. Let him be. It was the truth. The mention of plans reminded her that it was Friday night and she hadn't checked in with Brad yet that week. There was no need for Rancourt to know her plans consisted of finding a pay phone and calling her brother.

''Have fun,'' he said, maneuvering himself and the tray through the doorway.

''I always do,'' Olivia assured him enthusiastically.

He paused in the circle of light just outside. ''Better make it an early night. It may be the weekend, but around here breakfast is still at—''

Not caring that it was unspeakably rude of her, Olivia shut the door in his face. It was either that or lash out at him and let him see just how much he'd upset her. And that she refused to do.

Danby, she decided as she drove around aimlessly, had a serious shortage of pay phones. The only one she spotted was outside a service station already closed for the night. She probably should have known even before she climbed out of the car that the phone wouldn't work. She also should have known before she climbed back into the car that this would be one of the times it refused to start.

She had no idea of where she was, other than that it was miles from civilization. Faced with a choice between a long cold night in the car and a walk of indeterminable length, she convinced herself that the faint glow in the sky was the reflection from lights somewhere nearby and started hiking.

The lights turned out to be a hideous neon sign that read Sugar's in hot-pink letters at least six feet tall. Roadhouse was in smaller letters below it. The smaller letters flashed on one at a time until the entire word was lit, then they went out and did it over and over and over again. At the very bottom of the sign, the smallest letters of all promised Fine Food and Spirits.

''Yeah, right,'' muttered Olivia as she crossed the floodlit parking lot that was filled to overflowing, mostly with trucks and motorcycles. She hated walking in blind, but the only windows were well above eye level.

Here goes, she thought as she opened the door and was immediately sucked into a dark cocoon of music and loud laughter, sweat and smoke. The overheated air seemed to pulsate. The bodies paired up on the postage-stamp-size dance floor were definitely pulsating. She'd been to some rowdy bars and loud parties, but never any place quite like Sugar's Roadhouse. She could have used a crowbar to make her way through the crowd to where the phone was located outside of the unisex rest room in back.

There was an occasional catcall and whistle along the way, causing her to have second thoughts about calling

Brad. The loud laughter and music in the background would prompt questions, and she was in no mood to explain where she was or why. She finally decided to chance calling, reasoning that Brad was almost certain to be out at ten o'clock on a weekend night. Amazingly, she got lucky and reached his answering machine. Cupping her hand around the mouthpiece, she left a quick message telling him everything was just hunky-dory in Danby and that she would check in again next week.

Holding on to the receiver, she pressed the metal lever to get a dial tone and wondered whom she could call about her car. The obvious answer, Owen Rancourt, was out of the question. She would rather crawl all the way back to his place than ask him to come and rescue her. Besides, he had *plans* for the night. She rolled her eyes. She could call information…if she had any idea what listing to ask for…and assuming there was a service station in the county that didn't close when the streetlights came on.

"Think, think, think," she muttered to herself, closing her eyes and tapping the phone against her forehead as if she could jar loose a solution.

"Hey, hey, hey, little lady, you're going to go and hurt yourself if you keep that up."

She felt the phone being taken from her hand, smelled beer breath and opened her eyes to find herself face-to-face with Paul Bunyan. Or maybe Paul Bunyan's great-great-great-grandson. But the mountain of a man in front of her was definitely from a branch of the legendary lumberjack's family tree, from his red-plaid shirt and black suspenders to his booming voice and bushy rust-colored beard.

"Paul?" she ventured, thinking this was no weirder than most of her life recently.

"Nice to meet you, Paul," said the big man, grinning and pumping her hand. It was like shaking hands with a catcher's mitt. "I'm Sheldon. My friends call me Sid."

"I'm pleased to meet you, Sid." She was pleased. Sid looked like the kind of guy who would either have on him the stuff to jumpstart her car or know someone who did. She worked her hand free and shook it to get the blood flowing again. "But my name is—"

He jumped in. "Pauline, right? Pretty name for a pretty girl. Paul's pretty too, though. And less to write." He bumped her arm with his elbow. "Bet that's why you like it, right?"

Olivia gave up. "You got me. Tell me, Sid, do you happen to know of a service station near here that might be open?"

"At this time of night?" His eyes popped as if she'd asked him to run up to the bar and bring her back a glass of champagne and caviar on toast points. "Shucks, Paul, there's nothing open at this time of night... 'cept for Sugar's, of course."

"Of course." She shook her head dejectedly. "This just isn't my day."

"Aw, don't say that. Did you run out of gas or something?" They were both shouting to be heard over the din.

"Or something. I think my battery died. Do you think someone here might possibly be willing to try to start it for me? Naturally I would pay them for their trouble."

"Trouble?" A grin split his wide, amiable face. "You gotta be pulling my leg, Paul. I'll bet next week's pay there ain't a guy in the place who wouldn't pay *you* to let him jump your battery."

Olivia unleashed a dazzling smile, feeling as if the world had been righted on its axis. Of course these men would be willing, even eager, to help her. Had she allowed Rancourt to rattle her so much she forgot something so basic? It didn't matter. Everything was back to normal now, and she had Sid to thank.

"Heck, I'd do it myself if I had my truck with me. I'm not the designated driver tonight," he explained, holding aloft his bottle of Coor's light. "Hey, you want a beer? Or maybe a mixed drink? A cocktail? You come on over and have a seat and I'll get you a cocktail. One specialty of the house coming up." He was already pulling her along. "First I'll introduce you around and later we'll get someone to take care of you car. Where's it parked?"

"That way." She pointed. "I think."

Sid laughed. "Don't worry your little head. We'll find it." He stopped beside a table with people sitting two deep around it and banged his bottle on it several times to get their attention. "Listen up, everybody, this is Paul, short for Pauline. Paul, I'll start with that funny-looking fellow straight across from you. That's Ernie."

"Hi, Ernie," she said.

"Next to Ernie is his ex-wife, Loralee, next to Loralee is…"

He went around the whole table until the names and faces were a jumble in Olivia's head. They made room for her at the table, and she was quickly pulled into the light conversation that bounced around the group like a beach ball, changing direction without warning. Sid returned from the bar and placed a tall frosted glass topped with a paper umbrella in front of her.

"One Maximus for the lady."

"What's in it?" she asked, peering at the yellow-green liquid.

"Only Sugar knows," he told her. "She won't even let the other bartenders mix them when she's not here. No Sugar, no Maximus."

Olivia shrugged her shoulders and took a sip. The dry, smoky air had made her thirsty, and the sweet drink with its hint of pineapple went down easy.

"Is it okay?" Sid asked, hovering close by.

"It's great," she called to him and took another drink.

When he lifted his bottle and cried out "Hail Maximus," everyone within hearing followed suit, so Olivia did likewise. She soon caught on that drinking a toast to Maximus was a frequent occurrence at Sugar's, some kind of rural bonding ritual, she decided. Every so often someone raised his or her drink and called out the magic words and everybody chugged.

She was on her second Maximus, had lost count of the number of toasts and proved she could drink through a straw with a quarter balanced on her nose, when the lights blinked on and off and the crowd quieted. A woman with upswept auburn hair and a generous figure had replaced the band on stage. Flashes of light from the mirrored ball overhead made her flowing abstract-print tunic sparkle.

The crowd began to chant, "Su-gar, Su-gar, Su-gar." Jackie, the friendly woman sitting to Olivia's left, leaned over and explained that Friday night was open-mike night at Sugar's. Anyone who wanted to could get up onstage and take a turn at the mike, with Sugar's husband, Randy, accompanying, more or less, on the piano. When all the performances were through, the crowd had a chance to applaud their favorite. Whoever drew the loudest applause won fifty dollars and all the beer they could drink.

"What a great idea," Olivia heard herself say in a slightly slower and more melodious version of her usual voice. "That is such a really great idea."

Everything seemed to be a little slower and brighter and merrier. She felt as if she were floating and knew it must have something to do with Maximus. She refused a third, wanting to stay in complete control. That's why she could never figure out afterward exactly how it all happened. One minute she was laughing along with her new friends and the next she was standing in the spotlight with a cordless microphone in one hand and the tall, skinny man at the keyboard calling her Pauley and asking what she was going to sing.

She did later remember thinking it was lucky she wasn't shy, or a complete stranger to the spotlight. With four years of high school drama club and four of college behind her, she conferred briefly with Randy and launched into a song and skit that had been her contribution to the university's yearly Vaudeville production.

It was a loose rendition of an old French ballad about a woman who cannot find a man who pleases her, though she tries and tries and tries. The lyrics were French, but her comically risqué movements got the message across in any language. She finished to a standing ovation and, flushed and exhilarated, surrendered the stage to the next contestant.

She was too wound up to take a seat, so she watched from the sidelines and chatted with Sugar between acts. The bar's namesake was just as nice as everyone else there, and Olivia told her so. Several times. She felt so chummy so quickly, she even told Sugar the woeful series of events that had brought her there that night.

"You've got to be the dame who caused that whole mess with the bees," Sugar declared.

"You know about the bees?" Olivia asked, wishing she weren't standing so close to the speakers and could hear herself think.

"Sure. And about the thing with the coffee. It's all the talk in town." She chewed her bottom lip, getting red lipstick on her teeth. "So let me get this straight. This fellow you told me about, the one you made the play for and struck out...he's Owen Rancourt?"

Olivia nodded, and the other woman laughed so hard her rounded shoulders shook and her eyes watered.

"Oh, that is just priceless," she said, dabbing at them. She patted Olivia's arm. "Don't you take anything that man says to heart, hon. If I know Owen, he'll do a lot of stomping and snorting before this is over, but he's gone and picked himself a losing battle this time." She took Olivia's chin in her hand, turning her face to better catch the light, and smiled. "Oh, yes, indeedy."

After that, the night began to speed up around her while she continued in slow motion. First she was being called back on stage to accept first prize; next she was swimming through a sea of congratulations and back-slaps, trying to get back to her table. She felt like Miss America, or maybe Miss Roadhouse America. No, it was better than that. This was a prize she hadn't won with her looks alone. She stood in front of these people rumpled and without a speck of makeup, and never gave it a thought as she delivered her impromptu perfor-mance of a song she hadn't even thought about in years. Sure, she'd flubbed a few lines and hit a bad note here and there, but she'd made it work by laughing at herself.

And the crowd liked it. They liked *her*. Even without makeup.

When she reached the table, Sid stood and led a call of "Speech, speech."

"How does it feel to be number one going into the next round?" someone shouted.

She wrinkled her brow. "What next round?"

"Next Friday," a woman told her. "Same time, same place. The final round is the Friday after that."

"Oh, I don't know," said Olivia. "I never intended…"

"You're a shoo-in," the same woman insisted. "Trust me. I was here the night the winner was two guys in one cow suit, singing 'Country Roads,' a cappella."

"The prize money keeps going up," Sid added. "A hundred bucks for round two and five hundred for the grand prize."

"Don't forget all the beer you can drink," someone said.

Olivia mulled it over. "A hundred bucks for the next round, huh? What have I got to lose? I'll be here." Grinning and still clutching her winnings, she raised her fist in the air. "As for how I feel…I'm honored and I'm thrilled and…I'm buying!"

Everyone cheered wildly as she led the way to the bar and slapped down her prize money. As mugs of beer were being passed around, she climbed onto the nearest empty stool, folded her arms on the bar and rested her head on them, certain that if she could only close her eyes for a few moments, she would feel much better.

For the second time that day, when she opened her eyes the only thing in her line of vision was Owen Rancourt. Déjà vu all over again, she thought sleepily. The man did not look happy, and though she gave it her best shot, she couldn't blink him away.

She touched his arm experimentally with the tip of one finger. "You're really here, aren't you?"

"Yes. You're really sloshed, aren't you?"

"Not in the least. You take that back."

"How about if I just take you home instead?"

"I'm not ready to go home. Besides, how did you know where…"

He cut in. "Sugar called me."

"Well. She shouldn't have." The words came out a little bunched up. It occurred to her to lift her head from her folded arms. "I'm not ready to go and when I am ready, I have a ride."

"Yeah?" He looked around. "Where?"

Olivia looked around, too. The place was empty, the lights low, chairs stacked on tables. Even Sugar and Randy were staying out of the way, hovering over the books at the far end of the bar.

"Where did everybody go? Hey, Sugar, where's Sid?" she called.

Sugar looked up. "Gone home. He wanted to wake you, hon, said something about promising to fix your car. When he found out Owen was coming to claim you, he said to tell you he'll see you next Friday."

"Claim me?" She turned her head and looked straight at him, clenched her teeth and said it again, with feeling. "*Claim me?* If you think that I…uuuff."

She'd give the man this much, he was quick. And strong. And in spite of her squirming, he had her tossed over his shoulder in seconds flat.

"Consider yourself claimed," he growled.

The crisp, fresh air was a jolt to her senses.

"All right, Hercules," she said, trying to wiggle free. "You can put me down now."

His free hand landed on her backside and stayed there. "Why don't you shut up and enjoy the ride?"

She gave a disgusted huff. "I'll bet you're enjoying it."

"Sure am. How about you?"

"Not at all," she lied, very aware of the heat and weight of his hand, and of the little trills of excitement it caused inside her.

"That's too bad. Personally, there's nothing I love more than being dragged out of bed to rescue drunk women."

"I am not—"

"Drunk," he said. "You already told me."

"And you're not rescuing me, either. I wouldn't let you rescue me."

He yanked open the passenger-side door of his truck, rolled her onto the seat and stood with his arm propped on the roof. "Do me a favor, will you, lady? Next time you don't want me to rescue you, let me know *before* I get out of bed?"

The door slammed on her reply.

After they drove a few minutes, Olivia lowered her window to feel the wind on her face.

He swore and hit the brakes. "Are you going to be sick?"

"Of course not," she retorted, indignant. "I just wanted some fresh air."

The truck began to move again.

The night was dark and still all around them. On both sides of the road an early frost made tree branches and blades of grass appear to be dipped in silver. The effect was magical. The whole world felt wonderful to her, and she wanted to go on driving forever.

She really *was* sloshed.

"Nice night, isn't it?" she ventured, hoping to appear sober by making coherent conversation.

"Don't you mean nice *morning?*"

"Go ahead and growl, Rancourt. Not even you can ruin this night…last night. Whatever night it was." She waited a minute. "Aren't you going to ask me why?"

"I wasn't planning to."

"I'll tell you, anyway. I won the open-mike contest."

"I'm thrilled," he said in a monotone.

"No, you're not, but I am. Since you won't bother to ask what I won, I'll tell you that, too. I won fifty dollars and all the beer I could drink."

"That explains a lot."

Ignoring him, she continued. "And I get to compete again next week…for a hundred-dollar prize."

"I'll give you $125 to stay home and go to bed."

"Not a chance. I had no idea when I walked in how the night would end. I'm not even entirely sure how it happened, but it did happen and it feels great. You can't possibly understand what this means to me," she insisted.

Owen gave a quick sideways glance to see if she was putting him on. She wasn't. It couldn't have been the free beer that got her this excited. From talking to Sugar he knew she'd had only two drinks all night, some 90 percent booze concoction of Sugar's, meaning that two was plenty to account for the state she was in. More tipsy than drunk, but as a rule he didn't even like being around tipsy women, or men for that matter. It worried him that it wasn't the case with Olivia. It worried him more that he wasn't able to think of anything that would make him *not* want to be around her.

If the beer didn't do it for her, it had to be the money. That made some sense, considering that Doc Allison said Olivia had told her she needed a job desperately. Something to do with a family obligation. The only reason he'd taken her on was because he knew no one else in town would after she'd been fired a second time. It was a good thing he had, if she was willing to get on stage and make an ass of herself for fifty bucks. For all those lofty airs she put on, she obviously needed money even more than he thought.

Feeling a little guilty for the snide comments about her victory, he decided to make amends. "I was thinking," he said, "part of the prize ought to be some kind of trophy or certificate. That way you'd have something to remember it by."

"I don't need anything to help me remember. I know you won't understand this, but what happened tonight was like a small miracle in my life."

"Sure I understand. We all get caught short at one time or another."

His reassuring smile was met with a look of bewilderment.

"Caught short? You mean…financially? I don't believe it." She shook her head, a smile claiming her mouth. "You actually think I did it for the money."

"It's nothing to be ashamed of."

"Trust me, I'm not ashamed."

"I'm glad you can laugh about it."

"I'm laughing because it's funny. But in order for you to get the joke, I have to tell you a little secret."

"What kind of secret?" he asked, knowing she expected him to, and hoping like hell they made it home before she slipped into the irrational-crying-jag stage of intoxication.

He glanced her way as she twisted sideways on the seat so she was facing him. Something about her soft giggle and silly smile caught him off guard and slipped inside his chest to tug at his heart, every bit as urgently as her seductive beauty could tug at other parts of him.

"I'm an heiress," she said while Owen was still busy telling himself the feeling in his chest was meaningless.

He raised his eyebrows as he glanced quickly at her. "Would you mind running that by me again?"

"I said I'm an heiress."

She spoke slowly. It didn't help much.

"You know, an heiress," she repeated, that little pinprick of impatience in her voice. "A female who inherits—"

"Thanks, I have a handle on what an heiress is. Where are you going with this?"

"Nowhere," she retorted, the pinprick a little sharper. "I'm explaining why I laughed when you suggested I entered that contest to win the fifty-dollar prize."

"Didn't you?"

"No. Well, yes, in a way, but not because I needed the fifty dollars. Not in reality that is, only temporarily."

"Because you're an heiress."

"Exactly." She beamed at him.

"Okay, now I'll let you in on a little secret. Almost everyone inherits something at some time or another. That doesn't mean they'd turn down an extra fifty."

"Yes, I know everyone inherits something, but how many women inherit roughly a fifth of one of the largest combined fortunes in history?"

Silently he made the turn onto his property and covered the rest of the way more recklessly than usual. This promised to be a doozy and he wanted to give her his full attention while she laid it out. When he'd parked and turned off the engine, he put his back against the driver's door, met her gaze and waited.

She didn't disappoint him.

With minimal encouragement along the way, she explained how her father was the only son of the founder of what had grown to be an international corporation dealing in gathering, maintaining and supplying information.

"Basically it comes down to this, whenever someone runs a credit check or launches a hostile takeover of another company or starts a war, we make money," she explained. "Beyond that, I've never been interested enough to pay attention when my father and brothers talk shop."

"Makes sense." As much sense as anything else the woman said.

She went on to explain about her mother being fourth generation in a family of Swedish bakers who—surprise, surprise—expanded until they now manufactured and shipped packaged baked goods wherever sweet tooths existed.

"What's the name of the company?"

"Royal Confections," she responded without missing a beat.

He gave a nod of recognition. Of course he recognized the name. It was tantamount to him saying one of his ancestors struck oil in the backyard and, lo and behold, it turned into Exxon.

"Of course there's a lot more to it than that. There are divisions and subdivisions and one company is always buying or selling another, but that's what it's all built on. Information and pastry.''

"That sounds pretty incredible.''

"I know.''

"Just out of curiosity, with all those divisions and subdivisions scattered around the globe, they couldn't find a job for you anywhere?''

Her condescending chuckle would do any heiress proud.

"Of course they could. I could have whatever job I wanted, and nothing would thrill my parents more than my wanting one.'' A shadow fell across her lovely face. "Before he died, my grandfather—on my mother's side—went so far as to give me my own company. Just a small one. I guess he hoped it would motivate me to take an interest in business.'' She was looking past him, her smile wistful. "He gave me the Better Baker Cupcake Company, because that was his special nickname for me. Cupcake.'' She pressed her lips together and wiped what might have been a tear from the corner of her eye. "After that he would refer to me as the 'Cupcake Queen.'''

She was good, thought Owen. Almost frighteningly good.

Her deep sigh brought her bottom lip out an enticing bit. "I loved my grandfather, but…''

"I understand completely,'' he said when she trailed off, his expression was appropriately sincere. "You'd rather scrub floors than be the Cupcake Queen. Hell, who wouldn't understand a thing like that?''

"Don't be cute. Obviously, I would not rather scrub floors. Do you think I would be doing any of this…that I would even be in a place like Danby, for pity's sake, if I didn't have a gun to my head?''

That's when she told him about the wager with her brother, about throwing darts at some fancy charity shindig, about having to drive a strange car instead of her Jaguar and not being allowed something as basic as a cell phone. He would have sworn nothing could top the bit about the cupcake company, but this did.

Incredibly, the more she talked about this supposed wager, the more firmly her jaw became set and her tone more resentful. If he didn't know her, he could almost believe there actually was a wicked brother and a cupcake factory and a family fortune or two.

But he did know her.

"What would you do if something like this happened to you?" Olivia demanded.

Have myself committed, was his first thought.

"I really can't say off the top of my head," he replied instead. "Why don't you let me sleep on it?"

He didn't give her a chance to express the exasperation that flashed in her eyes. The woman did not like taking even a mild, barely recognizable version of no for an answer. With that subtle air of entitlement and the dismissive way she waved him off when he asked if she could make it to the cabin on her own, he could almost believe she was royalty.

Time and the night air might have sobered her some. As he walked her to her door, she seemed more tired than anything else. Not too tired to be trouble, however.

Before he could open the door, Olivia slipped in front of him, a fascinating, unpredictable gleam in her blue eyes, her wicked smile becoming more so as she moistened her bottom lip with her tongue. Desire flashed inside him, a hot, tense fist in his belly.

"Feel up to breaking your streak with a kiss good night?" It was more challenge than invitation.

Owen lifted his hand to the side of her face and stoked it gently, her skin so soft and warm it seemed to melt beneath his touch. "I would love to kiss you good night." His thumb drifted idly over her chin and under, where her skin was softer still. He lowered his head slowly, just until he heard her breath catch and saw her eyes flutter shut. "But I prefer my women sober."

Her eyes flashed open, a dark blaze of resentment already flaring in them. It was contained there while she unleashed a lethal smile and tiptoed her fingers up his chest, over the rough pounding of his heart.

"Am I one of your women, Rancourt?"

He couldn't help himself. He let his fingers slide deep in her hair, finding only more silk, more temptation. His voice was intentionally quiet and unintentionally husky. "Do you want to be?"

"I'm not sure," she drawled. "Maybe you could help me make up my mind?"

He moved his thumb to her mouth, caressing her lips, which trembled slightly and parted. He could feel her breath as she slowly dragged it in and let it go. He thought he could feel her pulse beating fast beneath his thumb, or maybe it was his own.

This was insane, thought Owen. He wanted her badly, had been wanting her for more than a week now. It could not be any clearer that she wanted the same thing he did. Part of him had already accepted that this was inevitable, and the part of him that was still resisting seemed to have forgotten why. What they were negotiating right now was simple, primordially so. No demands. No promises. Only heat, and that slow, deep, wet slide into oblivion. He could already feel the pull…the tightening of all the nerves in his body.

He moved his thumb until he found the moist heat just inside her parted lips. Her lashes drifted lower and she drew him in a little deeper, rubbing her tongue along the pad of his thumb. She sighed, murmured something he couldn't hear over the roaring inside his head and his control snapped.

It sounded like the clashing of swords. A surge of pure lust rocked him as he yanked her to him. It felt like going into battle, wanting and needing tangled together in a drive so intense it was as if his very life depended on carrying this through to the end.

After the barest flicker of surprise, Olivia was with him, wrapped around him, seeming to be inside his head somehow. His hands swept over her, molding her curves, her hips, her thighs, pressing her closer, closer. All the while her hands were racing over him with equal fervor.

He ran his hand down the side of her leg, up, around, in between. She gasped with surprise, with delight. Her own hands slid inside his sweater, running roughly over his back as she scattered kisses on his face and along the side of his jaw. He threw his head back, senses throbbing, braced, waiting for her to touch her tongue to his ear, grunting with pleasure when she did.

In an odd way, he seemed to know exactly where her hands and mouth would touch him next, and the seconds of anticipation beforehand added another layer of excitement. Even stranger, as his hands raced over her body, he had a sense that they were not exploring, but remembering. Each muscle, each soft hollow, was impossibly familiar.

Breathing hard, he shoved his hands under her sweater and pushed that ridiculous silky thing beneath out of his way so he could palm her breasts. Oh, no.

Even this was familiar, he thought, searching frantically for her lips inside a swirling cocoon of long fragrant hair and fractured breathing, needing hot, direct mouth-to-mouth contact to feed the need building in him.

She gave him what he needed and offered more. He wanted more, he wanted all of her, everything she would let him take. He sucked in her flavor, pulled her closer, wished he could pull her inside him, devour her and make her part of him. It wasn't a thought. It wasn't even desire. It just was.

That's when the part of him that had tried so hard to resist her remembered why this couldn't happen. How simple the reason was. He couldn't have Olivia because he wanted her too much, had wanted her too much from the instant he saw her. And he understood that if he allowed desire to override that resistance, if he crossed the line he had drawn a long time ago, his need would own him. Rule him. And he would never be able to survive without her.

Owen tugged down her sweater, then slammed his palms against the wall on either side of her head. It was the only way he knew to stop himself from touching her, from taking. He held himself still, willing his head to clear and his breathing to slow. The space he put between them didn't stop him from feeling her surprise move toward confusion. He heard her questions as they formed in her head and knew that, since he could never make her understand, it was better not to try.

When he was sure his voice was steady, he drew back and curved his lips into a smile she could interpret any way she liked. "Hope that helped."

"Oh, it helped," she retorted, seeming to have snapped back a lot faster than he was managing to. "Let me put it this way, if a comet were to drop on Earth this very second, and we were the only man and woman left alive, and the future of the entire human race depended on my decision, I still would not have the slightest interest in being one of *your women.*"

"That's probably a very wise decision." It wasn't the response she expected. Before she unfurrowed her brow and struck back, he pushed the door open and nudged her inside. "Get some sleep. It's hard enough to work all day with a hangover, without being exhausted, too."

He turned and took a step and then, like a kid who can't stop shoving a stick through the bars of the lion's cage, he glanced back over his shoulder at her.

"Just one more thing. You might want to lose that heiress routine. Folks already think you're a little—" he hesitated, feigned regret "—well, a little *off.* If that crap about being 'Queen of the Cupcakes' gets out, they'll laugh you out of town before you ever get a shot at that grand prize."

Chapter Seven

The sight of Rancourt standing at the stove, flipping pancakes and looking disgustingly energetic for the ungodly hour of 6:00 a.m., was enough to make Olivia wish she'd stayed in bed.

He glanced around when he heard her come in, his quick boyish grin taking her by surprise. *Boyish* was not a word she would ordinarily use to describe him, but this morning it fit. It wasn't just that elusive dimple, either. There was something about seeing him barefoot, clean-shaven, and with his dark wavy hair still damp from the shower that made her feel all warm and tingly inside.

For an instant it also made her forget the night before and that she loathed every fiber of the man's being.

Besides boyish, his smile was also amiable. As amiable as a good buddy. As amiable as if he had not tried to humiliate her last night and she had not bounced a hairbrush off his back as he walked away.

But, hey, if the man wanted to pretend none of it happened, it was more than all right with her.

"Morning," he greeted in a tone that matched his smile.

"Did you have to remind me?" With a wince she dropped into a seat at the table, where two white iron-stone plates had been set on black woven mats.

"What can I get you?" he asked.

"Aspirin. Extrastrength if you have them."

"I had in mind coffee, tea or juice, but two extra-strength aspirins it is."

The tablets materialized before her, accompanied by a glass of water and the appealing morning scent of soap and man.

"Thank you." She swallowed both at once and glanced up at him. "Did you say something about cof-fee?"

"I asked if you wanted a cup."

"Oh, please. Black."

"Be warned, I'm a little heavy-handed. It's been said my coffee can grow hair on your chest."

"This morning that's a risk I'm willing to take. Thanks," she added, accepting the mug he held out to her. First she closed her eyes and inhaled the aroma, then she sipped. "Perfect. Beyond perfect. Salvation."

"I like a woman with a strong stomach," he said, reclaiming the spatula.

His comment struck a chord in both of them simul-taneously. Their eyes met, looked away. The offhand reference to what he liked in a woman sparked flashes of the night before in her memory, the thrill of being pulled against him, all that heat and hunger, the sudden dizzying slip from consciousness to something else.

"How's your head?" he asked before the silence became too awkward.

"Just great. If not for the little guy pounding a hammer up there, I wouldn't be sure I was still alive."

"I've got to hand it to you for getting up in time for breakfast." Rancourt paused in the middle of transferring the golden-brown pancakes to a serving platter. "Or weren't you able to sleep after I left you last night?"

As if his implication wasn't sufficiently blunt, he paired it with a dark, mocking gaze that seemed to see all the way to her soul, while revealing nothing of his.

"Are you asking if I laid awake all night, pining for you and dreaming of what might have been?"

"Yes."

"No. In fact, I can't remember when I've slept as well. Nothing like hard work and fresh air for ensuring a good night's sleep, that's what I always say. When that alarm rang at five forty-five, I was up and raring to go."

"Five forty-five? Cutting it a little close, weren't you?"

"Not at all."

Arching one dark brow, he carried the platter to the table. "You always take only fifteen minutes to get ready in the morning?"

"Not always" Olivia conceded. "But you'd be amazed how much time you can save by cutting out makeup, blow drying your hair and your entire stretching and meditation ritual. Oh, and coffee in bed. I almost forgot that. Altogether I shaved nearly two hours off my previous best morning time."

"Damn, I hope these are worth the sacrifice," he said, sliding a third pancake onto her plate. "Maybe I should whip up a side dish of eggs Benedict just to make it worth your while."

Olivia touched his wrist to stop him from piling on a fourth. It stopped him, but it also caused another of those unsettling ripples in time where their gazes collided, clung and then pulled apart.

Staring at her plate, she said, "That's plenty, thanks. And thanks for the offer, but I don't think I could handle eggs anything this morning."

The quirk of his mouth suggested he understood and commiserated, and not for the first time Olivia found herself studying him as he served himself, wondering about all the things he didn't reveal as indifferently as most people did in the ordinary course of living. It was an interesting exercise, since she was accustomed to being on the receiving end of such fascination. And because he was not even close to the charming, cosmopolitan and wickedly handsome type she was attracted to. Or had always thought she was. A few weeks ago the man sitting across the table wouldn't have caused even a tiny blip on her radar screen. So how could something as insignificant as the way he poured maple syrup or chewed his food captivate her so completely?

"I've got no problem with you watching me," he said, the sound of his voice startling her, "but it isn't going to make you feel nearly as good as getting some food down yourself."

Her first thought was deny, deny, deny, but since her untouched plate underscored his point, she settled for shrugging and saying, "I thought I saw a glob of syrup dripping from the tip of your nose." As he lifted his napkin, she added, "But I was wrong."

"Thanks for being interested."

"It's the least I can do since you fixed breakfast…which, by the way, is right up there with last night's dinner."

"That's good, but you ought to know that the way it works around here is whoever doesn't cook, cleans up."

Olivia looked at the bowls and griddle and utensils scattered on the counter and wrinkled her nose.

He gestured toward her plate. "Eat up. There's plenty of batter left."

"You must be kidding. I'll be lucky to finish what's on my plate. If I'd been paying attention I would have stopped you after two."

"Two pancakes? That's it?"

"Two *giant* pancakes," she corrected.

"Well, at least that answers my question."

This time his nonchalant tone struck her as *too* nonchalant. She could smell a setup as well as any female with four impossible older brothers. She only wished she were half as good at resisting one as she was at sniffing it out.

"What question is that?" Olivia inquired.

"About why you're so skinny."

She gave a disparaging huff. "I am not skinny."

"If you say so."

"What do you say?"

He didn't look up from the syrup he was pouring on his second helping of pancakes. "I say skinny is in the eye of the beholder."

"And in your eyes I'm too skinny?"

Rancourt lifted a forkful of pancake and paused with it halfway to his mouth. "Maybe we better talk about something else."

"You know what I think? I think you go out of your way to provoke me."

"Could be." He swallowed. "But at least I'm willing to make an effort. For you, provoking me seems to be as natural as breathing."

"You're right, we should talk about something else." She glanced around as she chewed, silently admiring the streamlined look of the spacious kitchen, with its glazed granite countertops, white tile floor and oversize stainless steel appliances. "I'll bet you designed this kitchen yourself."

"How'd you guess?" he countered, sounding more intrigued than surprised.

"It reminds me of you. Simple and…" She caught the corner of her bottom lip and shook her head. "No. Simple is the wrong word. Practical, maybe, or straightforward. And efficient. And…what's the opposite of ostentatious?"

"Simple."

"All right, simple, but in an admirable way. I can't spot a single thing anywhere in here that's there for effect or to impress. You're the same way. Besides, the behemoth appliances and triple sink are a dead giveaway that this is a kitchen meant for serious cooking. And you," she added, saluting him with her raised fork, "are definitely a serious cook."

"The appliances are commercial grade…though I'm sure it's only because the manufacturer wasn't clever enough to come up with *behemoth*. And I chose them with serious cooking in mind, but not the sort you're referring to. When I run training sessions, I pay a local woman to handle the cooking and kitchen duty. That means three meals a day for ten to fifteen very healthy appetites…not counting the dogs."

"I can see why you went commercial. Does everyone eat here?"

"Yes, but usually only half at a time. Mrs. Benchly is worth twice what I pay her just for the way she schedules meals and gets everyone in and out on time. I'm working toward increasing the number of teams I can handle in each session. When I do, there'll have to be a separate building with a cafeteria and maybe a few pool tables for passing time at night. But that's still a couple of years away."

"How often are the sessions?"

"Six times a year, each session three weeks long."

"That's eighteen weeks out of fifty-two. What do you do the rest of the time?"

"I do a lot of one-on-one training for owners who can't get away for a three-week session or who don't have the patience to do it themselves. And I lecture."

"Lecture where?"

Shrugging, he reached for his coffee. "Wherever somebody's willing to pay my price. Usually it's law enforcement related."

Olivia put down her fork and wiped her mouth on her napkin, this one black-and-white-checked linen. "That's it. I surrender. And as much as I hate to admit it, you were right about eating. I do feel a little better."

"Let's see, by my count, that's at least three compliments you've paid me, and it's not even seven yet. You wouldn't be buttering me up so I'll go easy on you today, would you?"

"Would it work?"

"Probably not."

"Oh, well, you can't blame an indentured servant for trying. It's still a great kitchen."

Her approval seemed to please him. "Most of my

time and money has gone into getting the camp established. This and one bathroom are the only real reno-
vations to the house itself," he explained. "Except for
a coat of paint here and there, the rest is the same as
when I was growing up."

"You grew up in this house?" she asked.

"Yup." He immediately stood and began clearing
the table, his message clear: end of discussion.

Recalling what he'd said about the division of labor,
Olivia stood and looked around, wondering what she
was supposed to do first.

His hand landed on her shoulder to gently push her
back into her chair. "I'll handle it this time. Your turn
for kitchen duty will come soon enough," he assured
her. "After you've learned how things work and where
everything is kept."

He didn't have to twist her arm…which, like the rest
of her, was more sore today than yesterday. She grate-
fully accepted a refill on her coffee, thinking it was just
as well she stay out of his way. He rinsed the dishes
and loaded them into the dishwasher with no wasted
motion, the same way he didn't waste words when he
had something to say.

It seemed to Olivia a natural progression from watching him work to wondering if he also used the direct
approach when he took a woman to bed. Would he
make love in that deliberate, single-minded way? She
liked his hands. They were large, with broad palms, his
fingers long and agile. He handled the ironstone plates
with a sure and careful touch, in a way she could watch
for a long time without becoming bored.

He would be a very attentive lover, she decided, and
a shiver slipped along her spine at the thought of being
touched by his hands in that same mindful way, of being

the focus of his intense and undivided attention. Intense was good, very good, but would he also be patient with a woman? And generous?

That led almost inevitably to wondering what sort of woman would succeed with Rancourt where she was failing so abysmally in getting beyond the first kiss. Surely some woman must have. She'd done some calculating from the little he'd revealed about himself and figured out he had to be thirty or close to it. And he'd been in the military. All those base groupies. And then there was his body, which, to her annoyance, looked better to her every time she looked at it. In a bar, with the lights low and the music loud enough to drown out whatever he said wrong, he would be a real lady-killer.

Oh, yes, there must have been women. Regardless of how last night ended, his arousal had been too fast and too demanding for her to believe he'd be content to go without for too long. And as if all that weren't convincing enough, he just plain kissed like a man with a full past.

Engrossed in speculation about the women in that past, it took her a few seconds to realize that Rancourt was talking to her, and a few more to catch-up.

"So what do you think?" he asked.

"Think?"

"About running a few errands for me. I have to stick around and wait for a delivery of bricks for a wall I'll be building next week." He finished wiping the counter and tossed the sponge into the sink. "Of course, if you'd rather unload a few thousand bricks, I'll be more than…"

"I'd love to run errands for you, boss."

"I thought you might," he replied, his tone dry.

He explained what he wanted her to pick up and drop

off and where. She'd taken only a couple of steps when she stopped short.

"Oh, no." Olivia turned back to him. "I forgot. I don't have a car. It died on me last night. How could I forget a thing like that?" She scowled and waved off his patronizing look. "All right, I know *how*. That doesn't change the fact that I can't even remember where I left it. Someplace within walking distance of Sugar's, that's all I know."

He beckoned her to the window and pointed at the driveway.

"My car," she exclaimed, relief followed quickly by confusion. "How did it get home without me?"

He gave an incredulous shake of his head. "It didn't. Cars aren't like homing pigeons, you know. I saw it by the side of the road on my way to pick you up last night. Sugar had mentioned you had car trouble, so I called a buddy of mine who owns a tow truck and asked him to tow it back here first thing this morning."

"Thank you." Olivia frowned. "But how can I run errands if it doesn't work?"

"Run," he corrected with a pained expression. "Blenders work, cars run. And it's running fine at the moment because I had Manny throw a new battery in it. He thinks the starter might be on borrowed time, too, but it will be fine for today. First chance I get, I'll check it out for you."

"You can fix cars, too?" she queried, wondering why some people were useful in so many ways, and some not much use at all. Was it talent or discipline or simply being lucky enough to discover what you were meant to do with your life? Unbidden came the memory of the Christmas three of her four brothers had bought her the identical joke gift—three oversize coffee mugs with the slogan Born To Be Spoiled.

"I try," he replied. "But if you'd rather I not mess with it…"

"No, I'd be thrilled to have you mess with it…I mean, look at it. And grateful. Really. Just dock me whatever I owe you for the battery and any parts I need for the other problem, the starting thing you mentioned. I don't expect…"

"Olivia."

"Yes?"

"How about getting to work on those errands? Otherwise there won't even be enough in your pay to cover the cost of the tow."

"I'm on my way."

The rapid tap of her boot heels came to an abrupt halt when she spied a bundle of tan and blackish-brown fur curled up at the front door, dead center in a patch of sun-warmed tile.

"Romeo," she exclaimed, then looked to him for confirmation. "It is Romeo?"

"Sure is."

"Is he all right now?"

"He's doing okay," Rancourt replied, his smile unabashedly affectionate. The shepherd appeared a little stiff getting up, but his tail was wagging enthusiastically. He didn't look much like a bear to her today, more like a larger, more muscular version of Mac and Jez. Rancourt patted his side. "Glad to be home, aren't you, pal?"

Romeo responded by rubbing his head against his master's thigh.

"Doc said to let him take it easy for a while and he'll be fine."

"Thank goodness," Olivia said. "Have you heard any good news about Dan?"

"The hospital still has his condition listed as satisfactory, which doesn't mean a hell of a lot to me. He still can't have visitors, but that could change later in the week."

"I think about him all the time," she said. "Keep me posted when you hear something new, will you?"

"Definitely. Don't look so conscience-stricken. Anybody could have fallen into the hives and released those bees."

Olivia eyed him dubiously. "Do you really think so?"

"No," he admitted. "You're different from most people. You attract bizarre occurrences the way dogs attract fleas."

"I do like a sweet-talking man," she drawled.

"How about a truth-talking one? I'm not saying it wasn't a genuine accident—a freak accident, but an accident all the same. And beating yourself up about it won't do squat for Danny."

"I wish I could think of something that would…besides lying awake at night telling God all the things I will or won't do if He takes it easy on Danny." She absently reached to stroke Romeo's massive head and caught herself, her hand in midair.

"You don't suppose he remembers me, do you? And recognizes me as the person who…you know…" She lowered her voice. "The bees and all."

"You don't have to whisper. He hasn't mastered compound sentences yet. As for whether he recognizes you…" Rancourt gave the question serious thought. She expected at any minute he might stroke an imaginary beard for dramatic effect. "I'm sure he didn't take it lightly, being brought down by a woman and a bunch of honeybees. A skinny woman at that.''

She glared.

He smirked.

''Then again,'' he went on, ''Romeo's never been one to hold a grudge for long.''

''You do know you're a jerk?''

Ignoring that, he used the same ''Make nice'' command he'd used the first night to let Romeo know she was friend, not foe. Already more comfortable around the other dogs, she leaned down and lavished him with caresses, grimacing when she felt the many bumps where he'd been stung and telling him how sorry she was.

''When did he get home?'' she asked.

''I picked him up last night.''

''Last night?'' Even operating at morning-after speed, it took no time at all for her brain to click the pieces together. ''That was your big date? Picking up Romeo?''

He looked at her, one broad shoulder lifting carelessly. ''I never said anything about a date, big or otherwise.''

''Semantics, Rancourt. You said you had plans. Did those *plans* consist of picking up your dog and driving him home?''

''Romeo's not just any dog,'' he corrected, his placid tone indicating he was stating a fact and didn't much care if she agreed. ''But yes, that was my plan. While I was there I checked out some photos for Doc, and she gave me a copy of the application you filled out when she hired you. She figured it would save you having to fill out another.''

''That was very thoughtful.'' It was very *something,*

anyway, thought Olivia. "You two are pretty close friends, I take it." It would make perfect cosmic sense, she thought, if a female vet was the kind of woman he was attracted to.

"Close enough." He told Romeo to sit, pulled something out of his pocket and gave it to him. "Beef jerky," he explained. "I'm a better friend of her husband, Ben. He's a state trooper, heads one of their SAR teams. We've worked searches together, and Ben gives at least one workshop here each session."

"SAR stands for Search and Rescue, right?" Thank you, Gretchen, she thought when he nodded.

"Though River—that's Ben's dog—isn't only a tracker, any more than Romeo is." At the sound of his name, the dog looked up and was rewarded with a scratch behind the ears. "River is Ben's full-time partner on the job, so in addition to basic agility and scent work, he's also trained for protection and apprehension."

"Apprehension? As in apprehending a bad guy?"

"The PC word is *suspect,* but you have the idea."

"I've always wondered, how do you teach a dog to do something like that?" she asked, regarding Romeo with a bit of caution.

"You mean, how do you teach a dog to chase someone and bring him down, then bite and hold, using whatever force necessary, until he's given the command to release? We use volunteers. Remind me and I'll let you give it a try sometime."

"Thanks. I'll be sure to do that." She rolled her eyes, hoping it had been a joke. "Even with *volunteers,* it can't be easy to do."

"A lot of things in life aren't easy," he retorted, a sardonic slant to his mouth. "Ben finds it helps River to be involved in Schutzhund. In fact, the photos Allison wanted me to see were taken at a competition in Canada a few weeks ago. Ben's birthday is coming up and I've been giving her a guy's opinion on a scrapbook she's putting together to surprise him.''

That was probably what she'd wanted to show him the other day, too, Olivia decided, telling herself she should be ashamed for what she'd been thinking at the time.

''I'm sure that would strike me as a brilliant idea for a gift…if I knew what Schutzhund was.''

''It's part competition, part sport. It started in Germany around 1900 and spread across Europe, but it didn't really take off here till fairly recently. It's pretty grueling for the dog and handler. Once a dog qualifies to enter, there are three levels a team can achieve. They earn points by how well they perform the exercises at each level.''

''Exercises like what you did the other night in the yard?''

Rancourt shook his head. ''A novice exercise might be as simple as a dog heeling off lead, but it's a long way from there to the Master level, where a dog's given a time limit to scale a wall and retrieve something small, hidden on the other side by a stranger twenty-four hours earlier.''

She tilted her head to the side, curious. ''Why a stranger?''

''To replicate real life as closely as possible. On an actual search, a handler doesn't know ahead of time where to look, and a dog rarely has the advantage of tracking a scent he knows well.'' Before she had to ask, he smiled and added, ''And it's done ahead of time so the scent can age, the way a trail has usually sat awhile before you get to it.''

Olivia was pretty sure those were the most words she'd heard him string together yet. It was definitely the most open he'd been.

''Makes sense. Do you compete, too?''

''No. I do stick pretty close to their standards, though. They're the toughest around, and they're systematic. Training, obedience, protection. But that's as far as I take it,'' he told her, reaching down to stroke Romeo with an affectionate hand.

''So no blue ribbons for Romeo and the gang?'' she teased.

''I already told you, I don't need anyone else to tell me what my dogs are capable of, or a title and a ribbon to prove they're the best.'' A rare glint of humor appeared in his eyes. ''And I sure as hell don't need fifty bucks to prove nothing to a roomful of drunk strangers.''

''How about for fifty bucks and all the beer you can drink?'' she challenged.

''I'll pass on the beer, too.'' He pulled open the door and pointed the way out. ''If you still want to know more about Schutzhund, we can pick this up later, when you're on your own time.''

Owen couldn't say for sure why he'd gone so easy on her. If it had been Danny who'd gotten plastered, dragged him out of bed for a ride and shown up this morning blurry-eyed and moving at half speed, he would have leaned hard on him, if for no other reason than to make sure it didn't happen again in a hurry. He definitely would not have planned breakfast around his stomach, done KP duty for him afterward and then virtually given him the rest of the morning off.

Danny was not Olivia.

Dan was stronger, more experienced and worked harder. He also didn't talk too much or constantly get under a person's skin just by being there. Most of the time, if they were working in separate parts of the camp, Owen forgot there was even anyone else around. Never, not for a single instant, did he forget that Olivia was near.

It wasn't something he was happy about. In fact, he wasn't happy about a lot of things at the moment, starting with all that remained to be done before the fall session. If Dan had been where he should have been yesterday instead of in a hospital bed, the sandpit at the end of the east trail would be dug now, the ground leveled for the wall and the new dexterity run set up. And as for the damn cabins, they would wait until his regular cleaning service showed up. Just like always.

Of course, to be fair, Danny could never do some things that Olivia managed effortlessly. Only Olivia could keep him tossing and turning half the night simply by refusing to get out of his head. She could also drive every other thought and memory from his consciousness by melting against him and letting him ravage her mouth the way he had last night. The way he'd wanted to when she was sitting across from him at breakfast, sleepy-eyed, her hair loose and wavy around her face, gleaming like a hundred different shades of sunshine. The way he wanted to even now.

Last night had taken him by surprise. The speed and ferocity of his desire had made him rougher than he should have been. The proof was in the marks from his beard, still faintly visible this morning on her cheeks and the pale skin of her throat. When he saw them, he'd wanted to gather her in his arms and let his mouth soothe the damage he'd done—at least the damage that was visible.

He was far less willing to deal with a more subtle and potentially devastating injury, one that took a while longer to show up…years sometimes. But it was rooted in a feeling that had been tightly entwined with his raw need of the night before. *Feeling* was too innocuous a word. This was more like grabbing a hot wire with both hands. It was pure thrill ripping through you, blood roaring in your head, heart pumping with the swaggering, intoxicating rush that comes with taking what you want and making it your own.

Needing to wipe his mind clean and start fresh, he took Romeo outside and went through the motions of feeding all four dogs. While they ate, each at their own appointed place, he went inside and scribbled a note for the man bringing the bricks, asking him to lean on his horn when he got there so Owen could sign for the delivery. That way he wouldn't have to hang around the house waiting. As he grabbed the tape to stick the note to the front door, he noticed the envelope containing Olivia's job application sitting on top of a stack of mail where he'd tossed it last night.

He despised paperwork and invariably put it off as long as possible. So it wasn't conscientiousness that made him pick up the envelope. It also wasn't anything as mild as curiosity. He wasn't simply curious about Olivia; he wanted to know everything there was to know about her. He wanted to know things that couldn't possibly be written on a form, the way date of birth or educational background could be. What he wanted wasn't inside that envelope, but he was hungry enough for her to settle for whatever was available.

It was a short, simple, just-the-facts-ma'am style application. Even so, Olivia had skipped more questions than she'd answered. Maybe Doc had told her not to bother with anything but the basics. Maybe she hadn't. He could ask Doc, he supposed, but either way, he wouldn't know any more about Olivia than he did now. And the longer he stared at the damn thing, the more he wanted answers.

He hated gossip and made it a point never to stick his nose into other people's business. He'd lived through the curiosity and speculation that followed his mother's death and then, a few days later, his father's. He knew firsthand how it felt to be on the receiving end of rumors and nosy questions. But this was different, he told himself. As long as Olivia was living there and working for him, he had a right to know the truth about her.

Grabbing the phone, he punched in the number of the state police barracks where Ben was assigned. Through working with all levels of law enforcement, he had a number of contacts who would be willing to do him a favor. Ben was the one he trusted most, however. Ben wouldn't even tell Allison what he found out until he'd cleared it with Owen.

He explained to Ben what he wanted to know but not why, and wasn't surprised when his friend didn't ask. Fortunately, the information Ben needed to run a check on Olivia was on the application, her full name and address, as well as her Social Security number and Maryland driver's license number. Before hanging up, he assured Ben there was no hurry. Just the same, he found things to do that kept him near the phone. Ben.

wasn't one to let even a simple favor slide, and even sooner than Owen expected, the phone rang.

The first words out of Ben's mouth were, "Buddy, I hope you're sitting down."

What do you know, thought Owen, she really was the damn Cupcake Queen!

He listened to all Ben had found out, but he was already convinced that what Olivia told him in the truck last night was the truth, the complete, unbelievable and utterly baffling truth. She was an heiress. And someday, according to the biographical info Ben had turned up, she would be one of the richest women in the world.

He wasn't exactly a pauper himself. He'd been sole heir of his parents' estate, including the house and the twenty acres of valuable real estate it sat on. The camp was already a solid success and in between sessions, he had more requests for workshops and private training than he could handle. Barring an act of God, he had everything he would ever need. But what he had and what he needed were so far from the blueblood, industrial pioneer, social register wealth of Olivia's family, there wasn't a spreadsheet or pie chart in the world that could encompass both.

He understood that. Harder to get his brain around her reason for being in Danby. He knew what she *claimed* was the reason, and in a way, the story about her brother and the charity ball and the darts and shaving her head was so outrageous it had to be true. Besides, as hard as he tried, he couldn't come up with a single *normal* explanation for her being there, doing menial labor for a paycheck that wouldn't buy even one of the dozens of dresses he pictured hanging in her closet back home in Baltimore.

But even if he did buy her version of what she was

doing in Danby, he still didn't quite get why. People made stupid, impulsive wagers all the time. He once saw a fellow marine bet a classic Corvette on a game of improvised horseshoes in the barracks hallway. It was the single most idiotic thing he'd ever witnessed. But even that made more sense than this.

Having a few too many beers and acting on impulse was one thing. Doing it in the clear light of day was something else. Something a little mad. Who would actually upend their entire routine, move hundreds of miles from home and proceed to wreak havoc in the lives of everyone they came in contact with, just to prove a point? Who the hell had that much free time and money at their disposal? Who could possibly be that bored or pigheaded or self-indulgent?

Olivia, apparently.

He blew a long, slow breath through clenched teeth. What the hell could the woman be thinking of? Assuming she bothered to think at all, that is. From what he'd seen so far, Olivia was in no danger of being named poster child for the Look before You Leap movement.

On the contrary, she seemed dedicated to doing what she felt like doing, whenever and wherever she felt like doing it. Whether it was singing in a bar or throwing herself at a man who had the audacity not to turn into a quivering mass of nerves and hormones in her presence. Correction, he thought ruefully. Make that a man who refused to let her see she'd turned him into a quivering mass of nerves and hormones. It was as if she operated on the principle that she was the center of the universe and therefore her whims took precedence over everything else, including pesky things like the lives and welfare of everyone else.

The little brat had taken him in. The fact that she'd

told the truth and he refused to believe her was about as effective in soothing his ego as squeezing an eyedropper of water on a forest fire. No one else with half a brain would have believed her story, either…especially since she was half in the bag when she was telling it.

There was one bright spot. This slammed the door on any chance he might weaken and allow himself to fall under her spell. Olivia wasn't just the wrong woman for him, she was hands-down the worst choice of woman possible. From the moment he saw her, she'd made him feel and think and want things he'd promised himself he would never feel or think or want. And now it turned out she was also out of his price range.

How's that for irony, he reflected, he couldn't afford Olivia in every way there was. Make that Olivia *Templeton Ashfield,* he thought, giving in to a wry smile. It must be comforting to know that if you go through one fortune, you have another in reserve. Between the Templetons and Ashfields, he'd bet Olivia had always gotten everything her little heart desired.

So why stop now? He felt the tightness in his chest ease a little, and the first tantalizing traces of anticipation. Why the hell stop now? Olivia had come to Danby to prove herself, to prove she could survive on her own in the big cold real world, to show the world—at least her small, sheltered world—she could grind out a living side by side with poor working slobs whose lives were so different from hers they might as well live in another galaxy.

What right did he have to interfere with what the queen wanted? In fact, he thought, a smile spreading across his face, the decent thing to do was help her out a little. Olivia had her selfish little heart set on showing her fancy family and friends that she could tough it out against all odds. And he was going to see to it she did exactly that.

Chapter Eight

Driving into town, Olivia found a new appreciation for the expression *footloose and fancy-free*. With vintage Bruce Springsteen on the radio, she turned up the volume and sang along. She felt sixteen again, cutting class on a day too nice to waste indoors. She felt the same heady sense of exuberance and possibilities she'd felt as she and her friends slipped out the school's side door. Hearts pounding, they would make a crazy dash for a well-worn spot hidden amongst the cedars, where they would stretch out on the grass, smoke cigarettes and talk about boys.

Instead of escaping chemistry class, today she was breaking free of Owen Rancourt and his long list of chores guaranteed to make her aching muscles ache more. There was also another significant difference between then and now: her chemistry teacher never held the door open for her to make her escape. Rancourt had, and she couldn't help wondering why.

Even more bewildering was how she felt nearly as lighthearted on the return trip as she had making her getaway hours earlier. Only this time her mood had less to do with a reckless sense of freedom than it did anticipation. She wasn't quite sure how to describe what she was feeling, other than that it felt a little bit like Christmas Eve, and a little like waiting for a blind date to ring the doorbell and a little like coming home again after being gone a long, long time.

Excitement, suspense, comfort.

It was a strange mix, and potent. It must be to cause the persistent flutter in her chest and restlessness everywhere else in her body. There was no denying it, not to herself anyway. She was looking forward to seeing Rancourt again.

Good Lord, could that be her subconscious's way of telling her she'd missed him?

Olivia scoffed at the notion. Not possible.

It was more likely that she was mistaking her absence of dread for anticipation. After all, he had been unexpectedly tolerable at breakfast, almost pleasant, in fact. She thought wistfully of how much less stressful the coming weeks would be if he could only stay that way. It didn't require a Mensa member to figure out what had prompted *his* mood swing. It appeared that last night's kiss had not been the humiliating washout she'd first thought. Unless she was way off her game, the man was coming around.

Not that she had ever seriously doubted he would, she told herself. Now that his defenses had cracked slightly, all she had to do was disassemble what remained. Mingled with her satisfaction was a small twinge of something less comfortable. Scruples? Always before when she'd played this game, her opponent understood the rules as well as she did, and had his own bag of tricks. Owen Rancourt did not strike her as a man who viewed games as a diversion. If he played, he would play to win, no quarter given, none asked. That made them even, she decided, casting off any uncertainty.

In fact, she reflected, if you looked at the situation with an open mind, she was really performing an act of kindness by using the means at her disposal to motivate him to be nice to her. The sooner he cooperated and responded the way he was supposed to, the easier life would be for both of them.

The first thing she saw when she pulled up to the house was the load of bricks, thousands of them, neatly stacked on wooden pallets. Rancourt was nowhere in sight, but the barking coming from behind the house told her where to look first.

He was there, sitting in one of two dark green Adirondack chairs on the flagstone terrace adjacent to the house. She had about half a second after opening the gate to wave and tell herself that damn tingle running up her back was part of the thrill of the hunt and not the result of seeing him. Then all four dogs were galloping toward her at breakneck speed. Well, perhaps Romeo was galloping a bit more slowly than the others. When they reached her, however, he edged aside both Mac and Radar to get closer.

It was still a little intimidating to see them all rushing at her and surrounding her. These were not cuddly dogs or lap dogs or big lumbering pooches like the Saint Bernard down the street from her parents' house. Even

Radar, with his long bloodhound ears and woebegone expression, would never be accused of looking docile.

These dogs were warriors. That's all she could think as she observed the alert manner and leashed power unmistakable even when they were playing. No matter how friendly they may be at the moment, she understood that they answered to one master only, and would shift gears in a heartbeat to do whatever he commanded them to.

For the moment their master seemed content to let them socialize. He observed from across the spacious and well-tended yard awhile longer and then gave the command that summoned them to his side, taking time to reward each dog with a treat from his pocket and the touch of his hand.

Olivia purposely trailed behind, drinking in the sight of him as if she'd been gone for weeks instead of a few hours. There was something of the warrior in him, as well, she decided, that same intensity and tethered strength. She was suddenly very aware that he was a man who dominated his world, and that she had just stepped into it.

He may be sitting now, but it was apparent he'd spent the morning working hard enough to get his hands dirty, and to leave his shirt damp with sweat and his hair adorably mussed. She couldn't imagine any other man she knew looking as content to be right where he was. And *who* he was, she thought.

On the table beside him was a tall glass of iced tea with lemon. As she drew closer, her imagination conjured a different homecoming, with her leaning down to plant a quick kiss on his smile, a smile that said he was very glad she was there. Then the imaginary Olivia helped herself to a sip of his iced tea and collapsed in the other chair to tell him things about her day, and he listened, spellbound, as if nothing and no one was more important than her and what she had to say.

And all the while they sat talking, the air around them would hold that certain hum. Awareness of what that humming meant, and where it would lead, would pass from the deepening heat in his gaze to hers, lazily, the knowing making the waiting bearable, even pleasurable, no pressure, no doubts.

She wanted him. The realization was sudden and staggering. And it was the last thing she needed to have front and center in her mind at this strategic moment.

Don't try to make sense of it now, she told herself, wondering how she could possibly think of anything else when he was so close and everything she'd thought she felt about him—annoyed, disdainful, immune—had just been tossed and scattered as if no more substantial than a handful of confetti.

Smiling, she stepped onto the terrace and did what she always did when she didn't know what the hell she was doing: she pretended she did.

"Hi. Did you miss me?"

"As a matter of fact, I did." Rancourt stretched out his legs and linked his hands at the back of his neck to observe as she settled into the chair and curled her legs onto the seat. The day was one of those when fall seemed to stall for twenty-four hours and you knew you'd been blessed with one last chance to sit comfortably outside without a coat.

"I'll bet," she retorted. "I'll bet you worked up that sweat pining away over me."

He shook his head with a small smile of reproach. "You never learn, do you?"

"I guess not." Smiling, she scooped her hair off her shoulders and let it fall back. "Wanna teach me?"

"Somebody should have done that a long time ago. But since you're here, I suppose it's up to me."

"Poor baby." She executed a perfect pout and watched his gaze slide straight to her lips. "Would you be surprised to hear that I can name a few men who would jump at the chance to privately tutor me in…whatever it is you think I've never learned?"

"I'm sure you can name dozens, and that there are easily dozens more men whose names you don't know who'd be just as eager. That's how it works, isn't it, *cupcake?*"

She couldn't conceal her surprise completely, especially not with that shuttered gray gaze of his pinning her as if she were a lab specimen. So she had told him the truth last night. It wasn't simply a bad dream that had ended with him more or less calling her a liar, and a lousy one at that. That's when she hurled the brush at him. In the clear light of morning, however, she'd regained enough sense to realize that, dream or not, it was better all the way around to let him go on thinking of her that way. The truth would only complicate matters, she'd decided.

She'd been right.

"What are the odds you just happened to pull that name out of thin air?" she asked, her tone wry even as she was silently weighing how she ought to handle this.

"About the same as my happening to ask if you prefer to be called queenie, or maybe Your Highness. Is that what lights you up, sweetheart? A little bowing and scraping to go along with the drooling and pining away?"

"That was a joke," she claimed, referring to her earlier remark.

"This isn't. I don't like being lied to."

She shrugged impatiently. "I didn't lie…exactly. I simply left out a few details."

"Semantics."

"Was it semantics when I did tell you the truth and you refused to believe it?"

"No. That was a case of too little, too late. And I wouldn't have gotten that much if you hadn't gotten loaded."

"I was not loaded."

"You were close enough…cupcake. If you don't mind, I'll go with that one. I've never been real good at bowing and scraping."

"Really? Well, if it makes you feel better, you aren't doing a bang-up job of drooling or pining, either."

"There's that to be thankful for. And I suppose I ought to be grateful you didn't *accidentally* burn down the cabins while you were cleaning them."

"While I was cleaning all eight of them. And don't forget about painting all eight doors. Why don't you mention that along with all the things that have gone wrong for me?"

"What would be the point?"

"The point is that you wanted it done and I did it…to your great shock, as I recall. The point is that as long as I go on doing what you want done, it shouldn't matter to you who I am or why I'm here."

"Believe me, it doesn't. If you want to turn your life upside down, that's your business. Just don't think I'm going to let you do it to mine."

"I couldn't care less about your life," she snapped.

"Or anyone else's except your own."

"That's not true."

"Yeah? Prove it. Name the last thing you did that shows how much you care about someone's welfare besides your own."

He waited.

"How do you expect me to think with you staring at me with that know-it-all look on your face?"

"That's what I thought. But your character is your own problem, unless it interferes with me. Like now. As I was saying, if your life is so pointless that you can just walk away from it for weeks at a time because you got into a snit with your brother and you get it in your head to prove what a tough, resourceful princess you are—" he swung his arm out wide "—you go ahead and knock yourself out.

"Just remember this," he went on, managing to become more intimidating by softening his deep voice. "In order to prove yourself to them, you've first got to wake up every day and prove yourself to me."

"Wrong. I don't have to prove anything to you...and I don't intend to. The deal I made with my brother— who happens to be the youngest executive VP of the company he works for—"

"Who's the president?" he cut in.

"Does it matter?"

"It does if it's Daddy."

Rolling her eyes and waving her hand, she said, "Forget that. The terms we agreed on don't include anything about working for you...much less proving myself to you. Gainful employment, that's all that's required. I can work for whomever I please."

"In Danby."

"Right."

"Like who?"

"What?"

"Whom could you work for? After the fit you threw in the diner, and what's come to be known around town as 'that whole mess with the bees,' employers aren't likely to be lining up to offer you gainful employment."

"I'm sure there are—"

"Name one."

"I'd have to give it some thought."

"Let me save you the time. I'm the only one who'd take you on, and that's only because I was under duress when I did it. Face it. I've had to. We're stuck with each other."

Oh, how she wished she could turn on her heel and walk away. She wasn't sure why she hadn't already and worry about the consequences later. Maybe because he pushed buttons inside that even she couldn't override. The man had a lot of gall to stand there with that smug, superior smile and accuse her of being a spoiled, thoughtless princess. Just because she didn't walk around in sackcloth or punch a time clock did not mean she was a snob. And that's something she *was* willing to prove.

"You may be right. I'm not about to risk finding out, if it might mean losing."

"That's what I figured," he countered. It did not sound as if he was paying her a compliment. "So, as long as you're still on the payroll, it's time to work. Do you know how to mow a lawn?"

"I'm quite sure I can figure it out."

"Good. Come on."

She followed him around to the front of the house.

"There's an exercise field that needs cutting directly behind that second row of trees." He pointed toward some trees in the distance. "This should be the last cut of the season, and we use that field for jumps and agility training, so set the blade to mow it as close as possible.''

''You're the boss,'' she declared, walking in the direction he'd indicated.

He let her get a dozen or so steps before calling to her.

''Aren't you forgetting something?''

Tilting her head to one side, she tried to think what it could be.

''The lawnmower.''

Olivia hadn't noticed it was there until he reached for it. She regarded it hesitantly. ''That doesn't look like any lawnmower I've seen.''

''It's a push mower...does a nice close job.''

''What makes it go?''

He grinned and dragged it over to her. ''You do, cupcake.''

Halfway through mowing the huge field, she started sneezing and her nose began to run. Ordinarily she wasn't bothered by allergies. But then, ordinarily she didn't spend hours in a field of freshly mowed grass, surrounded by assorted other plants and mosses and unidentifiable growths.

Her nose wasn't the only body part weighing in with a protest. Her feet hurt; her back ached and her shoulder muscles spasmed every now and again. Even the palms of her hands hurt, with fresh blisters on top of yesterday's crop. Worse, she detected the beginnings of calluses.

She still refused to quit.

Her first glimpse of the field she was to mow had inspired a string of colorful comments on Rancourt's heart and his heritage. Then she cried, from anger and frustration and self-pity. When she finished crying, she glared at his stinking field and decided she would mow the damn thing if it killed her. At times she was sure it would. Every time the mower got caught on a large clump of grass, bucking and jabbing the wooden handles into her stomach, she cursed him again.

In between curses, she muttered to herself. You would think a man with all that land would invest in a decent lawnmower...one of those shiny red ones you could sit on and ride while it did the work. How much could one cost? Probably less than a weekend at her favorite spa. Unfortunately, that was more than she had access to at the moment. It occurred to her that it didn't matter whether a thing cost a hundred dollars or a few million if you didn't have enough in your pocket to buy it when you needed it. It was an aspect of shopping she'd never thought much about. Now she did, wondering what life was like when it was rent or groceries that were out of your price range.

After a few hours the field began looking like a desert, and the mirage dancing ahead of her no matter where she turned was not water, but a king-size bed. *That* was for her. For Rancourt she imagined wooden stocks like those used in colonial days. It was one of the milder punishments she dreamed of inflicting on him in order to break the monotony of trudging up and down, up and down.

She also started working on a survival plan, not just for that day but for every day she would have to—in his words—get up and prove herself to him. There was only one thing she had any interest in proving to him, and that was that he had met his match. He had some silly idea that she had taken him in, and his pride was wounded. To retaliate he was trying to turn her reason for being there against her.

He wanted to prove she *couldn't* make it on her own. He was out to break her, and she refused to break. Holding out was now her number-one objective; winning her wager with Brad and avoiding public humiliation would simply be the icing on the cake.

Plodding along, she tried to recall an article she'd read a while back. It was in one of those holistic magazines always lying around at the health club. It had captured her attention by promising a fail-proof method of finding serenity, happiness and your purpose in life. She couldn't remember the details, only that she'd snickered at the list of positive affirmations the author provided. At the time she'd wondered what kind of rocket scientist would believe that chanting could alter her energy patterns and change the course of her life. Now she was willing to try almost anything.

"I enjoy mowing grass in large open spaces belonging to conniving, two-faced madmen."

Well, it was an affirmation and the part about ownership was true, but it wasn't exactly positive and she did remember that the affirmations had to be positive and had to deal with the result you wanted to bring about. Something about intent forming reality, or was it the other way around? The basic idea was that if you acted the way you wanted to be, you would become that way.

"I enjoy working hard. Mowing grass is easy and fun for me. Sweat is good." *And I am insane,* she thought. "I enjoy hard work. Mowing grass is easy and fun for me. Sweat is good. I enjoy hard work. Mowing grass…"

* * *

Owen waited on the front porch for her to come slinking back. When a half-hour stretched to an hour, and then almost two, he began to worry that something was wrong. Was the woman pigheaded enough to keep going until she dropped? Without a doubt. The image of Olivia pinned to the ground under his father's old mower had him up and jogging toward the field.

When he neared the small rise above the field, he signaled the dogs to stay and went on alone, stopping as soon as he was able to see the exercise field below without being completely in the open himself. He shook his head, not sure whether to be pissed or amused to see half the field mowed and Olivia hard at work on the remainder. He watched her stumble when the mower snagged on something and then calmly reach down and clean off the blades before going on.

Damn it, she was going to stick it out and finish the job. The same way she'd cleaned all eight cabins in record time. And for the same reason...to spite him. Pampered and self-indulgent she may be, but she was also the most stubborn woman he'd ever known. And the most troublesome. Every time he figured he had her where he wanted her—more or less at his mercy—she twisted things around and found a way to be an even bigger pain in the neck.

She was a fighter. And he wasn't afraid of a fight. That and time were on his side. She was running on pure resentment right now, but he understood how resentment, like every other human emotion, didn't burn bright forever. Also, Olivia wasn't accustomed to more than eight hours of physical labor a day. Hell, she'd probably never even broken a sweat outside of aerobics class before. All he had to do was keep the pressure on and wait for her to wind down and wear out.

* * *

The next day was Sunday. Owen reluctantly bowed to her insistence that it was a day of rest and that he would burn in hell if he made her work. They compromised. He gave her the morning off and let her spend the afternoon doing her own laundry and cooking dinner for both of them. She made grilled cheese sandwiches, which, along with peanut butter and jelly, was the extent of her culinary repertoire.

He more than compensated for the lost time on Monday, keeping her hopping close to the house, raking, cleaning up the backyard and washing windows. Whenever she showed signs of flagging, he pushed a little harder. Ironically, rather than discouraging her as he intended, the more he leaned on her, the deeper she dug in her heels. He began to worry he might run out of things for her to do. Ostensibly she was there to fill in for Danny, but most of what he did was either too physical for her to handle or too critical for her to be trusted with.

The next morning Owen handed her a level and a shovel, and told her he wanted her to level the ground where he intended to build the brick wall. It took her the entire day, but she got it done right.

By Thursday he was running out of legitimate ways to wear her down. Over breakfast he ignored a small tug on his sympathy caused by the sleepiness in her eyes and the shadows below, and announced that it was Truck Day.

When her eyes narrowed warily, he drew her attention to the bucket he'd earlier filled to overflowing with sponges, rags, plastic bottles of window cleaner and whitewall cleaner.

When her knowing gaze sliced back to meet his, he grinned. "You do know how to use paste wax, don't you?

There were moments when Olivia questioned whether she would make it until Friday, which was Danny's day off and now hers. Her face was sunburned, her nails were a lost cause and she had as many cuts and scratches as in summers long ago, when she and the neighborhood boys raced through yards and vaulted over walls in late-night games of manhunt, their less civilized version of hide-and-seek.

There were other changes in her, as well, changes she couldn't examine in the mirror and gripe to herself about each night. Changes within. In a strange way, although aches continued to turn up in new places on her body, and Rancourt was piling on evermore strenuous and tedious chores, it was becoming easier to get through the day. She had never walked over burning coals, but it seemed to her that anyone who managed that feat would reach the end—with their feet burning like hell, of course—and look back knowing they had overcome not only the fire, but also something inside.

She felt a similar sense of accomplishment at the end of the day. And in the morning, after dragging herself out of bed and grumbling through a hurried shower, she was aware of a small ripple of exhilaration. The fact that the small ripple was engulfed in a riptide of dismay and self-pity did not make it any less real.

She had expected to derive immense pleasure from proving to Rancourt just how capable and tenacious she could be. She'd had no idea that it would be nearly as satisfying to prove it to herself.

All that pleasure and exhilaration aside, she was still elated when Friday arrived at last. She slept late, lingered in the shower until her fingertips started to wrinkle, and then dried off and propped her feet on the bed to paint her toenails candy-apple red. Every moment was filled with the awareness that she didn't have to rush or move or do anything she didn't want to do. It was a new slant on heaven.

In what she wistfully thought of as her "real life," almost all her time was free time. But trying to recall what she *did* with all that time produced a blur. There were no vivid details, almost as if it had also been a blur when it was happening, like something recorded on a faulty tape. For instance, she knew she'd painted her toenails countless times, but she couldn't actually remember even one of those occasions clearly, what song had been playing on the radio or the scent of the polish or how the cotton balls she used to separate her toes tickled them.

The lazy morning was such a pleasure, Olivia was almost sorry she had plans for the rest of the day. And for that night, she reminded herself. She was looking forward to open-mike night at Sugar's more than she'd expected. The only part of her usual routine she adhered to was stopping on the way to her car to visit Romeo and the other dogs. She wasn't sure they would miss her if she skipped a day, but she would miss them. That was another area where she was making progress: she had four of the five beasts she was living with eating out of her hand. The last one, she assured herself, was only a matter of time.

Olivia had called ahead to make sure Danny could have visitors and then stopped on her way to stock up on appropriate peace offerings. From Rancourt she'd learned that Danny was nineteen, lived with his folks—

who would prefer he be in college instead of working at a camp for dogs—and was a diehard sports fan.

The door to the room was open and she recognized the lanky, sandy-haired young man lying on the bed, watching the TV mounted on the opposite wall. There was an IV hooked up to his left arm.

"Hi, remember me?" she asked after a quick knock.

He turned at the sound of her voice, recognition coming to him quickly, followed just as quickly by awkwardness.

"You're the lady from the vet's, right?"

He was blushing, tugging at the sheet with one hand and straightening the collar of his pajamas with the other, Her heart went out to him. There were probably few things more embarrassing to a nineteen-year-old guy than being seen in striped pajamas.

"Darn it," said Olivia, shaking her head as she walked into the room. "I was hoping you wouldn't remember. Any chance you could pretend you don't and give me a second chance to make a first impression?" As he swallowed hard and bobbed his head, she reached into the shopping bag she was carrying. "My name is Olivia, by the way. Liv for short, and I come bearing gifts."

The stuffed black-and-yellow bumblebee she held up brought a genuine smile to his face. When she tossed it, he caught it with one hand.

"I hope he doesn't cause flashbacks or nightmares," she told him. "I just thought you could use a portable punching bag. Hospitals can get on your nerves pretty fast."

"A punching bag," he repeated, squeezing the bee. "That's pretty cool. I could use one around here."

"I figured. And I didn't want it to be me…not that

you wouldn't be justified if you took a swing." She touched his arm lightly. "I'm so sorry for what happened, Danny. I seem to have a knack for causing disasters lately, but you're the first person I've actually injured." With an uneasy frown, she added, "At least seriously. I did have a little…accident with some coffee, but it wasn't that hot and…"

His grin stretched ear to ear. "You're the lady who dumped coffee on Owen? I knew it. I knew it had to be you as soon as I saw you…not today but that day at the vet's."

"Figures he told you all about the crazy lady and the coffee. At least his version."

"He sure did. Only he didn't say you were crazy."

"Really?" Fascinated, she lifted her brows. "What *did* he say about me?"

"You won't tell him I told you?"

"Of course not."

"Because Owen doesn't like people talking about him behind his back. He doesn't like talking much at all."

"I've noticed."

"I think the only reason he said anything was because I razzed him about spilling all over his shirt and needing a bib." Looking thoughtful, he added, "And maybe because you were still so fresh on his mind."

"I'm sure that was it," she agreed, trying not to sound too eager and have him decide it was better to keep quiet. "So what did he say?"

"He told me what happened, and I asked what he did about it. He just sort of shrugged and said he did nothing. He said you were so beautiful you could probably get away with throwing just about anything at him. He said you were the kind of beautiful that makes it hard for a man to breathe." His head bobbed, revealing another spurt of awkwardness. "That's how I knew you were the one as soon as I saw you. You are that beautiful."

He was clearly not practiced in paying women compliments. That probably explained why the words struck such a deep chord in her heart.

"Thank you, Danny, that's a very sweet thing to say." To put him at ease, she quipped, "Though I'm pretty sure stopping your breathing with an allergy attack wasn't what he had in mind."

"Probably not. I was just so shocked when he did say it, I didn't think much about what he meant. Owen doesn't talk a lot about women. Not at all, really."

"Not what you'd call a ladies' man, hmm?"

"Oh, he's had plenty of ladies, just never the same one for very long."

She could think of at least a dozen more questions she'd love to ask, but didn't. She had her limits, and toying with a nice young guy like Danny was way beyond them.

"Okay, enough about your boss. I want to hear about you. Starting with how you're feeling."

She made herself comfortable on the edge of the bed while he told her about what he'd been through and how an infection he'd picked up in the emergency room had prolonged his stay and prevented him from having visitors for a while.

It eased her conscience a tiny bit when he explained that two good things had come out of the ordeal. He'd found out he was allergic to beestings and would carry an emergency kit with him from then on. And he'd decided to start college in the spring to study veterinary medicine.

"I've had a lot of time to think in here," he explained. "And it seems kind of a cool thing to be able to save a life, human or animal. It's just something I want to try."

"Then go for it," she told him. "Your folks must be happy."

He rolled his eyes. "My mom cried for, like, an hour when I told her."

"Sounds like a mom," she said, laughing along with him.

"Is she right about you filling in for me out at Owen's place?"

"Let's say I'm trying. You have my unending respect, Danny. That's a tough job...and having Simon Legree's evil twin for a boss doesn't make it any easier."

His sandy brows shot up in surprise. "Owen? You think he's a slave driver?"

"Don't you?"

"Well, no...not that's he's, like, a pushover," he rushed to add, as if torn between being loyal and being agreeable. "He's a straight shooter, and he's fair, and he's the kind of guy who you know would be there if you needed him. I guess I've always thought of him as sort of a big brother."

"You may be right," she allowed, thinking he did share a lot of her brothers' worst character traits. "But from where I stand, that's not always a compliment."

He pulled his mouth taut, as if fighting a smile. "Maybe it's, like, a guy thing. What'd he do to torque you off so bad?"

Was that what she was? *Torqued off* at Rancourt? Olivia wished the tangled mess of her feelings toward him were that simple.

She told Danny some of what she'd been doing as his replacement. His look of amazement and comical asides confirmed her suspicion that little, if any, of the work she was doing was part of his job. He didn't know Owen even owned a push mower, only a pair of super-charged ride-ons, and he'd never heard of Truck Day, much less been asked to scrub the whitewall tires with an old toothbrush. Unfortunately, he didn't have any sage advice for her, leaving Olivia torn between wanting to wipe the smugness off Rancourt's face by hanging in till the bitter end and proving she could take whatever he dished out, and wanting to wipe it off the second she got back by confronting him with the fact that he was playing dirty.

"I wish I could help," Danny told her.

"You did help. You listened to me whine," she said, checking her watch, then reaching for the shopping bag. "I have to leave soon, so let me show you what else I brought."

She piled an array of sports magazines and books on the bed as he thanked her repeatedly, stopping only when she threatened to take everything back if he thanked her once more.

"Oh, I almost forgot." She pulled a slightly battered bouquet from the bag. "These are for you, too. I figured wildflowers were appropriately manly, plus they were already in a vase. I wanted to bring candy, but I figured the way my luck is going, you'd develop a sudden allergy to chocolate."

"My mom brings me all kinds of candy," he assured her. "Nobody thought to bring me the *Big East Football Preview*. I didn't think it was even out yet. How did you know I wanted it?"

"The lady has a gift for that kind of thing," said a

deep voice behind her, drawing both her attention and Danny's.

Rancourt was standing with one shoulder resting on the doorway, his mouth curved in a suggestive smile that Danny might not understand, but she did.

"Olivia knows what every man wants," he stated. "Right, Olivia?"

Her smile was sweet, the look in her eyes anything but. "Sometimes better than the man himself."

"In which case, you're right and he's wrong?"

"You said it yourself, it's a gift. Some men are just clueless about what they really want. Others know, but they're afraid to admit it."

Their gazes, both wary, both defiant, clashed and held fast.

When Danny spoke, it sounded as if his voice was coming through a heavy fog.

"Hey, guys, remember me? I'm the *patient*…the one you're supposed to be here to see? Why do I feel like I'm missing something?"

Chapter Nine

Their gazes unlocked.

"Don't worry about it," Rancourt advised Danny, sauntering into the room. "Just try not to miss this." He raised a hand, gripping a package as if it were a football and feigning passing motions.

"Go long," he directed.

"Yeah, right," muttered Danny, but he stretched his arm as far back as space permitted.

Rancourt fired the package, making one of those peculiar male-bonding sounds when Danny snatched it out of the air. "Whoa, nice catch, kid."

After pretending to spike it, Danny opened the package and nodded approvingly.

"All right! Krispy Kremes. Who's hungry?" When they both declined, he shrugged and helped himself to one of the donuts. "Well, I am."

"When aren't you?" teased Rancourt. Shoving his

hands in the front pockets of his jeans, he shifted his attention to Olivia. "What are you doing here?"

"Leaving," she said smoothly and stood. "I have plans for tonight, remember?"

"Unfortunately," he said, not bothering to hide his disdain. "It's show time."

Ignoring him, she leaned down to brush sugar from Danny's mouth and kissed him. She touched his cheek lightly.

"You get better and get out of here," she ordered.

"I will," Danny promised, his smile silly and a little dazed from the unexpected kiss.

Owen understood the feeling all too well.

Both men watched her leave the room. She was wearing black boots and slacks, with a shiny black raincoat tossed over one arm. Owen had noticed right off that her pale-blue sweater was shorter and tighter than those she wore when she was working. In the past week he'd become an authority on the woman's wardrobe. It would be hard not to, looking at her as much as he did. All her sweaters looked soft and touchable, but this blue one might be his favorite. It made her eyes look even bluer, and hugged her curves in a way that made him ache to touch something he knew was even softer—the woman inside the sweater.

It had been a jolt to find her at the hospital. Several jolts, in fact. He hadn't expected her to spend her first time off in a week visiting a kid who, technically, she'd never even met. Knowing that she was short on cash, albeit temporarily, he wouldn't expect her to arrive with a Santa-size sack of presents for him. Knowing Olivia, he was stunned as hell she'd put so much thought and effort into making sure they were the perfect presents for Danny.

The biggest jolt of all, however, was the warm gushy feeling that went through him when he walked in and saw her perched on a corner of the bed, talking to Danny with an easiness that didn't exist between the two of them. It wasn't the first time he'd felt that rush of comfort and private joy, which, for that moment in time, made everything right with his world. He felt it when a search ended successfully and he was there to see parents, strung-out on worry, falling on their knees to embrace the child they'd nearly lost. Or a wife reunited with her husband, or a frail, befuddled grandfather, surrounded by several generations of family who cherished whatever pieces were left of the man he'd once been.

He'd felt that way for others but never for himself. He'd had no idea that a woman could come into his life and make him feel that way simply by existing. If he had, he would have closed himself off even more tightly to keep her out.

He couldn't say for sure how long he and Danny went on gaping in silence after she'd disappeared. He was just thankful Danny himself was so entranced he didn't notice he wasn't the only one.

Danny finally spoke first, absently touching the spot her lips had touched.

"Wow," he said. "Is she something or what?"

"Define *or what,*" Owen muttered, casually moving to the window so he might catch another glimpse of her walking to her car.

Evidently he did not manage it as casually as he'd thought. He swore he could *hear* the kid's know-it-all smirk even before he glanced over and saw it.

"So," Danny ventured, linking his hands at the back

of his head. "I hear Liv's filling in for me while I'm laid up."

Owen lifted one brow. "Liv?"

"Short for Olivia. She is helping you out, right?"

"I'm not sure *helping* is the right word, but she's around, for whatever that's worth."

"Hot damn." Danny shook his head. "Leave it to you, man. "

"What the hell is that supposed to mean?"

"It means you're a lucky bastard. Why couldn't *you* have been the one who got stung and me the one who gets to hang out with a woman like Liv?"

"Because there's a God," he retorted. "And—unlike you—God knows a woman like *Liv* would eat you alive."

"Not a problem," Danny declared. The gleam in his eyes revealed just how much he was enjoying this rare opportunity to yank his boss's chain. "At least not for me. I'm not so sure about you. Maybe that's why you're so uptight, and why you couldn't take your eyes off her when she was here. Maybe you're worried she might eat *you* alive."

Owen shot him a disparaging look. "Don't be an idiot. That's not what I'm afraid of."

"Then what—"

"Nothing, dammit."

"If you say so."

"I say so."

"Okeydokey, boss."

"If it's so okeydokey, what's that stupid grin for?"

"Nothing," Danny replied, his grin stretching. "Nothing at all."

"Good," Owen snapped. "Keep it that way."

* * *

The sky had been spitting and threatening rain all day, but it wasn't until late afternoon that it finally poured. The "slight chance of a thunderstorm" that had been forecast turned into a sure thing just as Owen arrived home.

He parked the truck beside Olivia's car, relieved to see she wasn't driving around in this downpour. It was really coming down now. Shielding his face from the rain with his hand, he checked out the sky and found it menacing in all directions. If it kept up, the weather might squelch her plans for that night. He couldn't pin down why it irritated him so much that she was hell-bent and happy about spending her time at a rowdy roadhouse, but it did.

Hearing a distant rumble made him think of the dogs, who were probably already hunkered down together inside their shelter, the "canine penthouse," as Danny referred to it. Every one of them would work in a storm if necessary, but given a choice, they'd opt to wait it out as far removed as possible from the thunder and lightning. He couldn't blame them, he thought, hunching his shoulders and picking up his pace. It was then he remembered the thirty-foot stretch of ground that Olivia had taken such pains to get perfectly level and he did a u-turn so that he was running away from the house.

The camp was laid out with natural landscape barriers separating the various exercise fields and training runs to minimize both audio and visual distractions. So it wasn't until he'd pushed his way through a triple row of wet arborvitaes that he saw Olivia struggling to do what *he* should have done before leaving to visit Dan. She was attempting to cover the freshly-turned earth with a green plastic tarp, and battling wind, rain and mud to do it.

Damn, he couldn't believe he'd screwed up. He never forgot things like this. It just wasn't like him. But his disbelief was overshadowed by his shock at seeing Olivia out there doing it for him. Hell, he was shocked it had even occurred to her that it needed covering, never mind that she'd gone to the trouble of finding tarps big enough and hauling them all the way from the storage shed. *That* just wasn't like her. At least, it wasn't like the woman he'd decided she was.

One look at the tarp flapping around her and he knew the first thing he had to do was anchor it on one end and go from there. Grabbing several good-size rocks, he dropped them a couple of yards from where Olivia was standing with her back to him, still trying to wrestle the airborne tarp to the ground. Lightning sliced the sky just as he reached out to touch her shoulder. She screamed, her eyes squeezed shut until he took her by the shoulders and shook her.

"It's me, Olivia. Open your eyes, for God's sake."

When she saw him, she swung out and batted his chest. "I thought I'd been hit by lightning." She whacked him again. "What the hell were you thinking, sneaking up on me that way?"

"That's the same question I was about to ask you. What the hell do you think you're doing standing in an open field in the middle of a damn thunderstorm?"

"What does it look like I'm doing?"

"You want to know what it looks like?" He was shouting to be heard over the storm. "It looks like you have a death wish."

"Only when you're around," she shouted back.

There was a rumble of thunder. From the sound of

it, the storm was a ways off, but he still didn't want her out there.

"Let go of it," he ordered when he tried to take the tarp from her and she immediately tightened her grip on it. "I'll take care of this. You get inside and dry off."

He was wet and cold and uncomfortable, but not so uncomfortable that he was unaware that she was even wetter and her clothes flimsier and the body they were plastered to much more interesting to look at than a patch of mud. If she only knew what an act of valor it was for him to tell her to go away when what he really wanted to do was drag her into his arms and let the tarp blow away instead. He would much rather do battle with her directly than continue the tug-of-war over a piece of plastic.

"I said give it to me," he shouted, annoyed that she was hanging on so tightly he had to strengthen his own grip.

"And I said no," she shouted back. "Go get your own."

"This is my own."

"Yeah? Well, possession is nine-tenths of the law, pal."

Capturing her wrist with one hand, he exerted enough pressure to make her yelp and loosen her hold. With his other hand he ripped the tarp away from her and used his shoulder and arm to fend off her attempts to get her hands on it again.

"Now it's in my possession," he declared. "So back off."

Her eyes, as dark as the sky, were brimming with annoyance and frustration. She refused to give up. When she failed to grab back her original tarp, she called him a name that could have been *guttersnipe* and could have been something much less flattering. Then she marched over to snatch another tarp from the pile several yards away.

"For God's sake, Olivia," he called after her. "Can you just this once make things easy?"

"No. Can you?"

He recognized the stubborn set of her jaw and said something that was unquestionably less flattering. "All right, all right. Do you want to help me?"

"No." Her chin inched higher. "But if you ask me real nice, I just might let *you* help *me.*"

He wanted to laugh, he wanted to punch something, he wanted to kiss her until neither one of them could breathe or think. He wanted her to go away so that his world could right itself and he could feel safe and steady again. He wanted her out of his system, one way or the other, whatever he had to do to make it happen.

"Olivia, may I please help you get this damn thing anchored down?"

"Why, Owen, how sweet of you to offer." She smiled serenely, managing to look beautiful in spite of the rain running off the tip of her perfect nose. When she realized he was staring at her, a cautious look came into her eyes. "What? Why are you looking at me that way?"

"You called me Owen."

"So? That's your name, isn't it?"

He nodded. "I'm just not used to hearing you say it. I like it."

"Swell," she snapped. "I'll call you Owen from now on. I just want to—" She flinched as the air crackled with lightning. The storm was moving closer now. "I just want to get this damn thing down and get inside. Got any bright ideas?''

He explained to her how they were going to do it. It took a while, and by the time they had the last tarp anchored in place, they were not only colder and wetter, but muddy as well.

She looked at him and laughed. ''Did anybody ever tell you that you look great in mud? It has a sort of an in your face, back-to-nature appeal. Definitely you.''

''Yeah?'' He wiped his hand on his thigh and took a step toward her. ''I'll bet it would look even better on you.'' He lunged, grabbing her and sliding his muddy palm across her cheek and chin before she managed to push it away. ''Let's see.''

He studied her face, his expression convincingly somber except for his eyes. For once they revealed to Olivia exactly what he was thinking.

''Sorry,'' he said. ''I'd like to return the compliment, but no dice. You're just not the mud type. Let me help you get it off.''

''No, I don't want your help.''

''Too bad, because I really want to do it.''

She was laughing too hard to fight him off, but she did her best to duck her head. He did better at forcing her face into the open by tipping her head back.

It was a primitive form of play, as old as man, as enticing as woman. Winding his hand through her long, wet hair, Owen tugged just hard enough to let her know he could. Inside his chest, his heart was pounding as wildly as any caveman's ever had. Olivia let him draw her back until her gaze met his, only inches separating them. And in that small space where their breath meshed, the air was hot enough to turn the rain to steam.

One second they were laughing, and then suddenly

they weren't. They were only breathing and holding on, both of them on the shaky edge of control.

"There's something else I really want to do," he told her. His slow, deep voice harbored both wonder and turmoil. "This."

His mouth took hers, dragging her into a hard, grinding kiss that made her knees weak. His teeth, his tongue, pushing, demanding.

Olivia trembled and melted, then rallied just enough to wind her arms around his neck to make him go on doing what he was doing to her, inside her, everywhere. She pressed close to him, going up on her toes, and when he broke away, his breath ragged and heaving, she ran her lips along his jaw and scattered rain-washed kisses over his throat.

He took her face in his hands. "I swore this wouldn't happen. I promised myself."

"I always knew it would. It had to. I felt it."

"I know," he said, nodding. "From the first time I saw you, when you threw coffee at me. I wanted you then." He pushed his hands roughly into her hair, his gaze moved to her lips and back, hot, hungry, ruthless. Excitement leaped inside her. "I want you more now, dammit."

"It's the same for me," Olivia told him.

His mouth tightened. "Is it? Do you even know what I want?"

"Tell me."

"All of you. Everything you'll give me. What you won't give me, I'll take."

"You won't have to."

He groaned softly and sampled her mouth again. "I'll give you back full measure," he told her. "Everything I can give, for as long as it lasts. Pleasure, that's what

I'm offering, Olivia, that's *all* I'm offering. And all I ever will.'' He ran one hand down her back, urging her body closer to his, making sure she understood his powerful need for her. "Is that enough for you?"

Olivia felt branded by his touch, every nerve in her body humming for more. "It is if it has to be."

He looked hard into her eyes, evidently seeing what he needed to see there, because he tightened his hold on her, brushing aside the hair the wind sent whipping across her face so he could again lay claim to her mouth. There was a flash of lightning, followed instantly by thunder so loud she wasn't sure if it was just her legs that were shaking or if the ground had actually trembled beneath them.

His embrace became fierce as he shielded her face against his chest. As loud as the thunder was, his heart was pounding even louder against her cheek.

"I must be crazy," he muttered, his laugh short and sardonic. "You must be crazier. Let's get the hell inside before I lose the rest of my senses."

He meant it literally, she discovered. As soon as they stepped into the house, the front door still swinging shut from the kick he'd given it, he whirled her around and pushed her back against the wall.

The breath whooshed out of her, and she had gulped only a little back when his mouth opened over hers and took that away, too. As his tongue drove her mad, he caught the bottom of her sweater and shoved it up, breaking the kiss only long enough to drag it over her head.

"Wet clothes," he murmured against her lips. "Gotta get 'em off…before you…catch cold."

"You, too." She clutched fabric, fumbled with buttons. "Oh, you, too."

His mouth kept her head pinned to the wall while his fingers searched wildly for a bra clasp that didn't exist. Before she could tell him so, he gave up and ripped it off. Then he levered the top half of his body away and looked at her and made a long, rough sound of delight.

His eyes were all the colors of the sky outside, heavy-lidded with passion. He slid his hands under her breasts, cupped them and stroked his thumbs back and forth across the tips. Already affected by the cold, they tightened more as he went on touching and caressing her, sending currents of pleasure shooting to every part of her body. Olivia had never felt so alive, so aware of every sliver of sensation, so unaware of everything that wasn't him.

He kept it up until the excitement became excruciating, like nothing in her past experience. The thought of just how limited that experience was shot through her mind and was gone. She had never felt that her lack of sexual experience was a liability, and now she wasn't feeling it at all. She felt only sure of herself...sure of this moment and this man. And ready for him. They were feelings as new to her as all the others Owen had awakened with his skilled and savage seduction. It was more than she'd imagined it was possible to feel, almost too much to take without relief.

Relief teased when his hands lowered to open the zipper on her slacks. Hooking his fingers inside the waistband, he tried to slide them down. When he met the resistance of wet fabric on wet skin, he growled with frustration, and with one arm holding her steady, jerked them to her ankles. Clinging to his broad shoulders for balance, she kicked them aside, along with her boots and socks.

It was the first time she'd ever stood completely naked in front of a man and allowed him to devour her with eyes that scorched wherever they touched. The first time for a lot of things, she thought without trepidation. The first time she had ever been dizzy with wanting a man. She was frantic to touch Owen the way he was touching her. His hands were everywhere at once, it seemed, with the urgency of a man who can't get enough.

Desire and impatience welled up higher and higher inside her until it was an effort to breathe. The need to feel his body against hers made her as greedy as he was, shattering any trace of self-control. After waiting so long for this moment, and this man, the last thing she intended to do was control herself, or hide how badly she wanted him.

"I want this off," she demanded, grasping the front of his shirt. Her voice was ragged, her fingers trembling and clumsy as they jerked open buttons. "Help me. Please."

Owen shrugged out of the shirt and used it to quickly wipe the last traces of mud and rain from first her face and then his own. Tossing the shirt aside, he reached for his belt buckle and watched as she watched him get rid of the rest of his clothes. Olivia's contribution to the process was to run her fingers, and then her mouth, over his chest, and trail her hands up and down his arms, thrilled by the texture and the taste of his skin, loving the hard muscle and rough hair and occasional scar that made him male and so splendidly different from her.

Yet another first, this a stunning one, was being pulled close and having every inch of her body skin to skin with his. She was amazed at how perfectly their bodies fitted together, awed by the tethered strength in him, excited beyond reason to discover that, in spite of his strength and all those muscles, she could make him tremble and moan by sliding her palm along the hardest, hottest part of him.

His own palms, rough and calloused, moved down her back, from her shoulders to her thighs. His head bent and he raked kisses along the side of her throat before crushing his mouth to hers and devouring her.

The kiss went on and on. His hands roamed freely, teasing and tormenting her. When at last he slipped one hand between her thighs to cup her, the contact jolted them both. She shuddered, her body restless and yearning. Sensations, all of them new and explosive, poured through her. He was all she could feel. When she breathed, she tasted him. When she gasped, he swallowed the sound.

Olivia was conscious of how the raw energy in him was coiling tighter and tighter, and she knew the instant his control finally shattered. She sensed the torrent inside him a heartbeat before he grasped her waist and with a harsh groan, lifted her, turning so that it was his back against the wall, his strong arms supporting her as she instinctively wrapped her legs around him and let him guide her down, onto him, around him.

Now, she thought, all willingness and need as his hot flesh pressed against her. *Now.* Clinging to him, she gave herself up to the relentless downward pressure of his hands. Now he would take.

There was only the slightest bit of resistance, a flash of trepidation in the storm-gray eyes that found and held hers, a flicker of discomfiture. Then there was only heat, roaring through her, flooding and slowly filling her, all of her, places she had never known were empty. When he thrust all the way inside her, she cried out, not with pain, but wonderment.

The sensations licking at her grew more intense and urgent as his movements became faster and deeper. With each stroke she felt the exquisite climb of pleasure, tangled with a need that was mindless and ruthless and primitive. Intimacy was raised to a daunting level because everything she felt, she was also able to see reflected in his eyes.

His gaze never strayed from hers. When her own blurred and began to drift, he nipped her bottom lip. "No. Stay with me, Liv."

She stayed, and was engulfed in the sensation of being possessed by him, body and soul.

His breathing became harder and faster, his grip on her hips tightened, and all she could do was match his rhythm and hold on. The same way her body had sensed it when his control broke, it now recognized the dark vicious flash inside that rocked him, dragging his head to her shoulder, his eyelids falling heavily, as he filled her with his heat, surrendering to her in the most fundamental way possible, giving what he'd vowed he wouldn't, couldn't—himself.

It was surrender without defeat or victory. This was about something else, something that was also uncharted water for her. Her eyes opened wide.

Was she in love with him?

Oh, yes, she thought, still dazzled, still shimmering. Oh, yes, of course. It made such perfect sense that if she weren't so worn-out from working, she would have realized she was falling in love.

Gradually Owen brought his panting under control. Slowly he allowed her body to slide down his until her feet touched the floor. Reluctantly he opened his eyes and faced the damning reality of what he was pretty sure had just happened. Of what he had *let* happen.

They had barely stepped inside when he was on her like a rutting bull, no thought given to finesse or consequences. He'd never treated a woman so thoughtlessly or with such an absolute lack of anything resembling tenderness. Never. The fact that she had been just as eager and every bit as hungry for it was beside the point. It was his own code he had violated.

And that wasn't the worst of it. The gnawing fear of what might be the worst of it was lodged like a hundred pound boulder in the center of his chest.

There was no easy way out of it, and no graceful way to go about asking what he needed to know in order to deal with it. At least none he was able to think of with the aftershocks of good sex pumping through him and his body still drenched with the scent and feel of her.

"There's something I have to know, Olivia. Are you... I mean, were you...?"

She gazed up at him with those impossibly blue eyes and a smile that made him want to kiss her, hard, and do it all over again.

"A virgin," she said matter-of-factly. "Is that the word you're fumbling for?"

"It'll do," he retorted.

"In that case, the answer is 'no' to the 'are you' part of the question, and 'yes' to the 'were you' part of it."

He closed his eyes. It was hard enough to think straight without riddles. Still, it took only a few seconds to figure out what she meant, and it quickly wiped everything else from his mind.

"For God's sake, Olivia, did it ever occur to you that you should have let me know a thing like that upfront?"

"Yes."

"Then why the hell didn't you?"

"Because I was afraid you'd stop."

"You got that right. I *would* have stopped." He grimaced and shook his head. "Maybe I would have. I know I *should* have stopped. As soon as I even suspected you…" He dragged his fingers through his hair, teeth snapping together with contempt, all of it aimed at himself. "I told myself you couldn't possibly be a virgin, that it didn't matter anyway, that it was your call and I'd stop just as soon as you said to. In other words, I told myself whatever it took to keep from letting you go."

"Thank God," she murmured, dipping to plant a kiss at the base of his throat. "I hate it when you make me beg."

Her mouth felt good on him. *Too* good.

He took her face in his hands, struck by the delicacy of her bones, and stared hard at her to see the results of what he had done. What he saw was a woman who seemed to shine even in the storm-dimmed light, a woman more warm and vibrant and desirable than ever. The only discernible difference was that the self-assurance he was so accustomed to seeing in her eyes now had a fiery edge of excitement…and challenge. Definitely not the look of a woman with a heart full of regrets. Nor the look of a satisfied woman, he noted with a pang of conscience.

"I was so rough with you. And so impatient…and much too fast." Saying it drove it home with a sledge-hammer, making him feel mortified as well as sleazy. "I am so sorry, Olivia."

"I'm not," she retorted, tossing her hair from her face. "If rough and impatient and fast feels that good, I can't wait until you slow down and take it nice and easy on me."

He shook his head. "I don't get it. You're not only beautiful, you're sexy, beyond sexy, you're the hottest damn woman I've ever known."

"Really?" she said, her smile edging toward wicked as she ran her hands up his chest, feathering her fingers through the wedge of dark hair bisecting it.

"Really. If you were any hotter, I'd be a dead man. The question is...well, there are a few questions I need answered. I want to know, how does a woman with no experience get that hot? And how the hell did you stay a virgin until the ripe old age of...?" His heart stalled. "Tell me you're not a mature-looking sixteen."

"Relax," she soothed, laughing. "I'm twenty-four, not even close to being jail bait."

"That makes me feel about a half a millimeter less of a bastard," he declared with self-condemning wryness. "No matter how old a woman is, her first lover shouldn't do such a lousy job."

"I don't think you're a bastard, Owen. I think you're incredible."

He grabbed her wrists to halt the distracting movement of her hands. "Cut it out...at least until you finish answering my questions."

"Finish asking them."

"Okay, last one, two parts. Why now? Why me?"

"In order," she began. "Hot is in the eye of the beholder, but I've never believed that having sex appeal requires me to jump into bed simply because I'm curious or drunk or because it's expected of me for one reason or another. It means much more than that to me.

"As for why I've never made love with anyone else," she continued, "it's pretty simple. I never wanted to. Today, with you, I wanted to."

"Just that simple?" he challenged, warning himself not to read too much into her explanation.

"Just that simple." She shot him a cocky smile. "In case you haven't noticed, I always do what I want to do, when I want to do it."

"Trust me, I've noticed."

"So does that answer all your questions?"

"Actually, you confused things more."

"That's too bad. Because I don't feel like answering questions now. The second half of my guiding principle for life is that I never, ever do anything I don't want to do."

"That's not exactly a surprise, either," he drawled.

She slipped her hands free and linked them at the back of his neck, pressing close to him. His blood stirred.

"Ask me what I do feel like doing now," she instructed.

He shook his head, slowly running his hands down the sides of her body and telling himself he was a very weak man to want her again, so badly, so soon. "No."

Her playful pout provided an irresistible reason to slide his tongue across her full lower lip. "Mmm…why not?" she asked.

"Because it's time someone taught you that there's an exception to every guiding principle of life." Without giving her time to react, he swept her into his arms and turned toward his bedroom. "In this case, it means you don't get to have your way until I'm done having mine."

Chapter Ten

It wasn't only anticipation that flashed in Olivia's eyes as he carried her to his bed. It was lust, clean, honest lust. And it was all it took to send fresh heat searing though him.

He should feel guilty, Owen told himself, falling onto the bed so that her body would land covering his and they could wrestle for the top-dog position until he decided to end it and savor the pleasure of having her under him, watching her on the long, slow slide from feisty to warm, sweet putty. He should feel callous, and opportunistic, and the epitome of every rotten quality attributed to the male gender since the dawn of time.

He didn't. Unlike the last time, he felt tender and patient and determined to take all the time he needed to show her how good nice and easy could feel when it was done right. With his own desire banked, he was free to devote himself to all the hidden places and undiscovered pleasure points he had overlooked earlier.

Her response was instantaneous and explosive. She quivered beneath his slow-moving fingers, twisted restlessly in his arms and tried desperately to get him to do the one thing he refused to do, which was hurry. He had promised to give back in full measure what she gave to him. He'd had no way of knowing the extent of that promise. Or how very much he would want to fulfill every nuance of it.

He wanted to give her everything, show her everything, teach her everything. Until Olivia, he'd never been the first for a woman, and as much as part of him regretted taking what he had no right to claim, another part of him gloried in the knowledge that no other man had ever touched her or loved her this way. It was important to him that she remember that—that she remember *him*. So he explored and worshiped every amazing inch of her. He felt invincible at it because she made him feel that way, every time she moaned or arched her hips or looked at him with her eyes full of wonder, glazed with passion.

The more he gave, the more he found he needed to give. The more aroused she became, the more he wanted to spin it out. The more she surrendered, the deeper he wanted to take her…to take them both. He didn't expect to get caught in the back draft of his own careful seduction. He didn't know he would end up racing with her, beside her, *inside* her, in that last desperate rush to mindlessness. He felt her climax in velvet waves that tightened around him, engulfing him in a warm, wet fire that roared past his last shred of restraint and kept him with her as she fell and fell.

It was good, so good he couldn't lift his head to tell

her so for several dazed moments. When he could, all he was able to manage was a ragged, disjointed mutter that seemed to please her madly.

She lifted her hands to his face, her ivory skin flushed from sex, her lips swollen, the look on her face suggesting she was beholding the greatest of all life's treasures.

"It's you," she breathed, her tone soft and incredulous. "It's always been you."

"Mmm," he agreed, happy in his current state to agree with just about anything. Nuzzling her neck, he rolled his weight off her, pulled her into the crook of his body, ready to let the sweet bliss of inertia take him away.

"I think I'm in love with you."

He opened his eyes and propped up on one elbow to see her face, taking no comfort in the look he saw there, the one that said she was certain she was right and anyone who disagreed—everyone in the world if it came to it—was wrong.

"No," he said firmly. "You're not."

"You're right. I don't think I love you. I know I do."

Every warning and reason he'd ever heard about avoiding virgins came rushing back.

"And don't kid yourself that it's only my lost virginity talking," she advised in a tone that was droll and calm, a lot calmer than he felt. "Because it's not that at all."

"Conventional wisdom would say it is."

"It would be wrong. I'm not exactly the conventional type," she pointed out. "Why would this be different?"

"Because it *is* different," he insisted, sitting up and reaching for a cigarette before remembering he'd quit smoking over a year ago. He sublimated by standing and grabbing a dry pair of jeans from the closet. He didn't feel any less exposed with them on.

"Can I borrow a shirt?" Olivia inquired, stacking pillows against the sturdy, black iron headboard.

He pulled a dark-plaid flannel shirt from his drawer and held it while she slipped into it. When she went to button it, he moved her hands out of the way and did it for her. Finished, he hunkered down by the side of the bed and took her chin in his hand, stroking his thumb back and forth across her bottom lip.

"Olivia, sweetheart, I know you don't realize it now, but this has been a crazy day for you. It's natural for you to be overwhelmed—"

"I am not overwhelmed," she broke in to announce, following up by touching his thumb with the tip of her tongue. "I'm happy, and I'm very satisfied, and I'm in love, but I am not overwhelmed, at least not overwhelmed enough to hallucinate."

"How about enough to confuse what you're feeling with something else?"

"No. Listen to me, Owen, just because I was a virgin doesn't mean my experience with men has been limited to holding hands and a good-night kiss at the front door. I've led a very full and interesting life."

He couldn't stop himself. "How interesting?"

"Tell you what, you make a list of all the names and activities in your past. I'll do the same, and we'll swap."

"Forget it," he growled. "I'm probably better off not knowing."

"Ditto." She grinned. "Maybe I should have given more thought to timing before I told you. But it just came out. When I was a little girl, my mother told me the story of how she met my father at her sorority's winter ball, and how she knew the moment he touched her hand to lead her to the dance floor that he was the man she would marry and love forever. One of the things that kept me a virgin all those years was how sure I was that it would be that way for me, too, that when the time, and the man, were right, I would know it. No doubts. No second thoughts."

Olivia brushed the hair from his forehead. While she was speaking, her grin had softened into something more tender. "So when it happened just that way, I couldn't keep it inside."

He shifted his weight, resting his forearms on his thighs. The right words didn't exist, so he searched for any that would make her understand. "Listen to me, Olivia. I'm not your father." He gestured at the room around them. "This isn't a sorority ball. And no matter how it seems to you now, I promise that you are not going to love me forever."

She smiled. "Fine."

"Fine? What does that mean?"

"It means you're free to think whatever pleases you, and I'm free to do the same."

"Damn it, Olivia." He shot to his feet and stalked across the room before turning to face her, and found himself struggling to keep his thoughts in order while she was curled up in his bed, doing for flannel what Jennifer Lopez had done for plunging necklines. "I don't want to hurt you. Ever. But I feel an obligation to tell you that I will never love you."

She was completely unruffled by the news, which left him slightly miffed.

"I think what you're really saying is that you'll never admit that you love me, not even to yourself." Her expression grew thoughtful. "Maybe especially to yourself."

"That's not it at all."

"Then explain to me what it is," she prodded, stretching out her long legs and crossing them at her ankles where the twinkle of her gold ankle bracelet drew his attention, reminding him how she felt and tasted at that very spot.

Throwing a muzzle on his imagination, he dropped into the old leather chair he used for reading and hitched his leg over one of its rounded arms.

"Love, with or without the marriage and forever angle, isn't part of my future plans. In fact, it's not even within the realm of possibility."

"Why?"

"Why?"

She nodded.

Why? He raked his fingers through his hair, wishing now for a cigarette *and* a drink…something he swore off long before he quit smoking.

"I told you that this is something I never talk about. And I meant it. But it might be the only way to convince you to quit while you're ahead where I'm concerned. I owe you that much."

Carefully choosing a place to rest his hands so he wouldn't fidget nervously or punch something, he said, "You asked me how I ended up on my own at fourteen. That's how old I was when my mother fell down the cellar stairs and broke her neck." He saw that he'd jolted her and went on. "My father died a few months later. He shot himself in the head when he found out the county prosecutor was about to file charges against him for the murder of my mother."

Olivia rose to her knees. Before she could move any

closer, he was out of the chair and pacing, praying she would read his body language and stay away. It was hard just to think about all this. Talking about it was hell. Having someone—especially Olivia—offer comfort would threaten a wall it had taken him years to build.

"I'm sorry," she said from the bed. "I'm sorry it happened. Sorry I asked. Sorry I made you feel you owed me an explanation. You can stop now. I understand. I don't need the details."

"You need a few," he told her with a rueful look, hands shoved in the pockets of his unsnapped jeans. He stretched his mouth into a smile. "Relax, I'm not going to go psycho on you. I got my feelings about it under control a long time ago." His smile faded. "And that's just how I intend to keep it."

He lifted a hinged silver frame from the top of a pine chest of drawers and handed it to her before reclaiming his seat. Olivia remained kneeling, but rested her weight on her feet to look at the photographs of his parents. Together. Smiling. The way he had decided to remember them. Even if there were other things he couldn't afford to forget.

"My mother was beautiful," he told her.

She nodded, staring at the photo of a young woman with short blond hair and huge brown eyes. "Very beautiful. Great cheekbones."

A smile flickered across his face. "Great mother." He paused. "My father was a charmer, friends with everybody he met. The life of the party. And a drunk."

He pressed his lips together, surprised it could still hurt so much after so many years. Olivia waited.

"I loved them both," he went on. "And I always knew they loved me. I thought I had a perfect family.

I figured everybody's dad smelled like gin every night after dinner and occasionally shoved their mother around and dumped his dinner on the floor and stormed out of the house. And called her a whore.''

He wasn't looking at her now. It wasn't necessary that he chart her reaction to each new horror, only that he lay it out for her so she could see she was holding a losing hand if she was counting on him to be the prince in her fairy-tale life.

"Of course, as I got older and spent more time at my friends' houses, I started to figure out that it wasn't normal after all. And I started trying to read his mood when he walked through the door at night, and forestall the worst of the scenes any way I could. When I couldn't, I'd find a way to get him so pissed off at me that he'd leave my mother alone.'' He took a breath, wanting to skate along the surface of the memories so they couldn't pull him back under. It had been too hard to climb out the first time.

"But I still loved him. When he was sober, he was a great dad and a great husband. The night my mother died wasn't one of those times. He was already half in the bag when he walked in the door. I was the only sophomore to make the varsity basketball team at school and we had a game that night. I loved for him to come and watch me play…unless he'd been drinking. Then I dreaded it. He'd yell at the refs, the coach, the other team.'' He hunched his shoulders. "I hated it. And when it was happening, I hated him.''

"That's understandable.''

"So I've been told. That night I would have done anything to get him to stay home. So I told him exactly how I felt. I told him he was a loser, and that I didn't want people thinking I was a loser, too, because I got stuck with him for a father. I told him I couldn't wait for the day my mother smartened up and realized she deserved a lot better and left him.''

"It was an away game," he continued. "And all the way there on the bus I had a sick feeling in my stomach. I knew I had really pushed his buttons this time. I wanted to throw up in the locker room, but I was embarrassed. What I really wanted was to go home and make sure everything was all right."

He took a deep breath, wanting it over quickly now. "At halftime the coach took me into an empty office. A couple of cops were already in there. They told me what happened and that my mother had been taken to the hospital. They didn't say she was already dead. They didn't have to. I knew it. I knew the second the coach tapped my shoulder and said he wanted to talk to me."

"Oh, Owen, I can't even imagine what that was like for you. God, you were only a kid."

"But about to grow up in a hurry," he added with a grimly philosophical shrug.

"Were the police right?" she asked quietly. "Did your father have anything to do with it?"

"I don't know. I'll never know." Memories, lined up like dominoes waiting to fall, brought a bitter smile to his face. "Afterward, at his funeral, several crazy aunts on that side of the family took pains to tell me that it was more proof of the Rancourt family curse."

"They think your family is cursed?" she asked, looking politely skeptical.

"It's all right to laugh. They also think dropping a spoon will bring visitors and throwing salt over your shoulder will bring luck. And that dogs don't belong in the house," he added sardonically.

"Silly them. What kind of curse do they say it is?"

He made a dismissive gesture. "Some rot about booze and brawls, and how Rancourt men always destroy what they love most."

"You don't believe any of that?"

"Of course not."

She looked hard at him. "You do. You do believe it…that's what this is all about."

"Don't be stupid. Here's what I believe. He said she fell. The investigators said there was no way she could have landed the way she did unless someone had pushed her backward. Nobody who knows what really happened is around to say."

Owen suddenly felt weary. "All I know is that from the moment she died, my father was a mess, drinking around the clock, crying. Half of what he said made no sense at all. It was a toss up whether it was grief or guilt that made him shoot himself. I punched holes in a lot of walls and lost more sleep than I got before I accepted that I wasn't ever going to know for sure, and learned to let it go."

"Is that a joke?" she asked.

"Why? Is it funny?"

"Not especially. It's just such a blatant lie I was sure you couldn't be serious."

He exploded. "You think I'm lying to you about all this? What for? To get out of saying I love you?"

"I don't think you're lying to me at all," she returned, her attention on the methodic rolling back of the shirt sleeves that were a good six inches longer than her arms. "You're much too busy lying to yourself."

"That's a cheap shot."

"No, it's not. It's a fact…and you need to hear it."

Olivia swung her feet to the floor. Owen tensed, but

she didn't approach him as he expected her to do. Instead she squared off opposite him and folded her arms across her chest.

"How can you possibly think that you've let it go, or moved on, or whatever else you tell yourself, when this obviously dominates your life?"

"It doesn't—"

"It does so. It dictates what you can and can't do, whom you can and can't love. You said it yourself, even your future is ruled by your feelings about this horrible tragedy...your *unresolved* feelings, I should add."

"I don't have any unresolved feelings," he bit out. "I resolved them just fine a long time ago. Long before I even knew there was a Cupcake Queen. I don't drink. And I don't fall in love. End of story."

"The hell it is," she declared. "You are not your father, Owen."

"That's right, I'm not. I don't take chances with other people's lives."

"I don't consider it— Don't you dare walk away." When he kept walking, she kicked up the volume. "Wuss."

Owen stopped, not sure whether to laugh or wrestle her to the ground and stuff a sock in her mouth. He turned and looked at her, all sex-mussed hair and long bare legs. "What did you call me?"

"Wuss. I called you a wuss."

"Take it back." He took a step toward her and watched the wheels in her head spin. "Take it back, Olivia."

Only Olivia could shrug with such defiance, he thought.

"Okay, I take it back. You're not a wuss...but it did get your attention."

''Is that what you're after? My attention? Because if it is, all you have to do is get rid of that shirt and I'll give you all the attention you can handle.''

She tilted her head so she was looking at him through a flutter of long dark lashes and made a show of considering his proposition. It was an adorably kittenish performance. Unfortunately, he wasn't in the mood to play nice.

''Take off the shirt, Olivia.''

She tossed her hair back, raised her eyebrows and pursed her lips. ''Make me.''

The buttons that had been on the shirt were still rolling around on the wood floor when he tossed her flat on her back on the bed and moved over her.

''You're going to have to learn to sew,'' he told her, stretching her arms above her head.

''One of us is,'' she countered, shivering with pleasure as his teeth found the sensitive tip of her breast.

''Oh, yes,'' he uttered when he reached down and found her already wet and ready.

''Oh, yes,'' she echoed when he plunged inside her with one powerful stroke.

Owen's brain fogged over. He remembered they had just had their first argument as lovers, but not whether he had won or lost. Not really caring, he nudged her thighs apart to go even deeper, pressed openmouthed kisses between her breasts and up the side of her slender throat, and turned her face so he was looking into her half-closed eyes.

''I don't love you,'' he whispered.

Olivia smiled. ''Prove it.''

They were about halfway to Sugar's place. The storm had passed and the lingering rain was only a fine mist glazing the windshield of the truck. An Elvis Costello CD was playing quietly, and every so often the wipers fanned over and back.

"It's not too late to take me up on my offer," said Owen.

"What offer is that?"

"A hundred twenty-five bucks to skip tonight's contest and come home with me. That's twenty-five more than the prize money," he reminded her.

"What about the beer?"

He shot her a sexy grin. "I'm sure I can come up with a suitable substitute."

"Yes, I'm sure you can. I'm still going to pass."

Without saying a word, they had settled into a comfortable truce following their earlier clash. Olivia understood that the lull was temporary. The bumps in the road between them were too big to ignore. He didn't understand her enthusiasm for open-mike night. She didn't buy his reason for insisting they restrict themselves to, at best, a platonic friendship with some bone-shattering sex mixed in and, at worst, a meaningless fling.

Their truce couldn't last. It didn't matter. She liked the way Owen fought. Clean and head-on, and when it was over, it was over. She did the same. The way the man made up wasn't too hard to take, either, she mused contentedly. She considered it a very good sign that they were so much in sync on both fronts. It was an indication that if they wanted to, they could overcome any obstacle. She definitely wanted to, and Owen might not realize it yet, but he wanted it, too.

She could have easily given in and skipped open-mike night. As much as she'd been looking forward to competing tonight, staying home with Owen was also tempting. She just didn't think it was good for either of them to start doing—or not doing—something simply to placate the other.

Besides, she had her heart set on winning the whole thing.

"Last chance to save your pride," he advised, after parking and shutting off the truck's engine.

"You don't give up very gracefully, do you?"

"I could ask you the same thing."

"I think we've already established that."

He chuckled. "True."

"Of course, if it's your pride you're worried about, you have a choice. Are you sure you want to be here?"

"No. But I'm sure I don't want you getting tipsy and driving home in the rain on narrow, winding roads."

"My hero."

"Don't start," Owen growled and got out, circling around to open her door.

Almost as much as he didn't want her driving home, he didn't want to sit home alone wondering how many come-ons she was fending off. The thought of some guy hanging all over her rankled him. More than it should. More than he should allow it to. Unfortunately, a glitch had developed in his ability to convert his knowledge of what *should* happen and of what he *should* allow into action. Otherwise, there would be a lot of souls in hell chipping away at icicles as he set foot inside Sugar's, with Friday night in full swing.

As soon as they stepped inside, people started popping up and waving and calling out invitations for Olivia to join them. At least, Owen hoped it was Olivia they were waving at, because she was sure waving back, not to mention greeting most of them by name and playfully blowing a damn kiss in acknowledgment of some overly enthusiastic hooting and hollering.

It was a good thing he'd come, he decided, discouraging the stares of the men close by with the kind of menacing glare that was hardwired into the male psyche, as was their deferential response.

They understood that Olivia was his by virtue of the fact that she had walked in with him. His hand was resting on the small of her back as if he had every right to put it there, when in fact, he had less right than any man in the place. He acknowledged that even if Olivia refused to.

Just for tonight, however, none of that mattered. Tonight she needed him...another fact she would no doubt be loath to admit. She needed what his heart already ached to give her...and what his head told him he couldn't risk offering. Just for tonight he would take care of her and slay her dragons and pretend he loved her.

He felt justified when he noticed that at least one man was immune to his menacing demeanor. He recognized the big man hurrying toward them as Sid Morse, and since Sid outweighed him by at least a hundred pounds, he was secretly relieved when he greeted Olivia with only brotherly affection.

"You had us worried, Paulie," he said after he'd released her from an enthusiastic bear hug. "We worried you had car problems or just decided not to come." There was a hint of shyness in his smile as he added, "We sort of feel that with you, we've got a dog in this fight, if you know what I mean. Seeing as how you sat at our table. We saved your seat, so come on. You can come too, Owen," he tacked on. "Always room for one more, right, Paulie?"

"Right, Sid." As Sid cleared a path for them, Olivia glanced over her shoulder at him. "Just go along with the name thing, okay?"

"Why?"

"Because it began as a mix-up and I let it go and I don't want anyone to think I was making fun of them and…well…" She paused, bristling under his amused regard. "And if you must know, Pauline has a lot to do with why I came back again. I'd like to get to know that side of myself a little better. Now are you coming or not?"

He made a small, sweeping motion with his arm. "After you…Paulie."

Chapter Eleven

The phone rang.

Eyes shut, his face nestled in the soft, warm, fragrant crook of Olivia's neck, Owen dragged his hand from under her pillow to lift the receiver and grunt hello.

"Who is this?" demanded an unfriendly and unfamiliar male voice.

"Apparently not the guy you're looking for." The receiver made it six inches from his ear before the angry voice pouring out of it prompted Owen to pull it back.

"Wanna repeat that?" he asked.

"No. But I will. I said I'm not looking for a 'guy' at all. I'm calling to speak to my sister. Since this is the number she left for me, I naturally assumed I could reach her at it."

"Did you assume that before or after you decided it was all right to call someone at—" He opened one eye to check the clock. "Damn. Never mind."

They'd overslept. Again. With good reason. In the week since he'd first made love to Olivia, they'd been acting like teenagers. Or newlyweds. Teenage newlyweds who'd adopted the motto Use It or Lose It.

He was worn-out and happy and more or less awake, now that he had a suspicion who the irritated man on the phone might be.

"Whoa, whoa," he said to stop the litany of complaints and accusations pouring into his ear. "Nobody's giving you the runaround, pal. If you'll just shut up for half a minute, I could ask you what your sister's name is."

"Oh, no," moaned a sleepy sounding Olivia.

"Olivia," the caller snapped. "Her name is Olivia."

"I'm not here," she whispered.

"Is she there or not?"

Olivia came alive enough to use sign language to warn him that if he didn't say what she told him to say, he would be sorry.

"I'm not sure," he stalled, trying to think of the sign language to ask what was in it for him if he did say what she wanted. "Describe her."

He could hear the steam pouring from the guy on the other end. Her brother Brad, he decided. Had to be. And after listening to her stories about growing up with four big brothers, he had no qualms about torturing this one on Olivia's behalf.

"She's about five-seven, slender, blond…"

"Beautiful?" Owen interrupted.

"Very."

"Long legs?"

"I've never measured them," he replied in an icy tone. "And if you have, I strongly suggest you keep it to yourself."

"Point taken," Owen agreed, his grin causing Olivia to roll her eyes in disgust. "Tell me, does your sister Olivia talk a lot and tend to sputter when she doesn't get her own way?"

Owen thought he detected a snort of laughter just before the reply. "So she is there. Put her on the phone, please."

He held out the receiver. "It's for you."

"Tell him I'm not here. Tell him I'm in the shower. No, tell him I'm outside working. Hard. Tell him I'm working hard."

"I can't remember all that," he said around a yawn. "You tell him."

Irritated with men in general and these two in particular, Olivia snatched the phone from his hand. "Hello."

"Olivia?"

"Brad?"

"Yes," they said at the same time.

"What the hell is going on there?"

"Why on earth are you calling me now?"

"Voice mail…message…telephone number…any of that jog your memory?"

"I'd jog your brain, if you had one," she retorted. "I seem to recall leaving a time frame for return calls, and this isn't it."

"Sorry. I only listened as far as the number. I figured I'd hear the rest when I called."

"Okay, listen up. The message was 'I'm fine, you're still a pain in the ass, tell Mom not to worry, I'll call you next week.'"

"I think I got it all. Now tell me about the joker who answered the phone."

"There's nothing to tell."

"Don't try to snow me, Liv."

She heaved a long-suffering sigh and considered what she could tell him to get him to back off. It wasn't easy to do with Owen's warm, clever mouth busy at the side of her throat.

"His name is Owen Rancourt. He runs a camp here in Danby. And I've been working for him for a few weeks now."

"Doing what? It sounds to me like the two of you just woke up."

"Really, Brad. Get your mind out of the gutter."

Owen slid his tongue lower.

"It's not what's on my mind that concerns me, Liv. Are you living there at this guy's camp?"

"Yes. There are separate cabins for the…camp counselors," she told him.

"How many counselors are there, besides you?"

"Let's see…I have my own cabin and there are one, two, three…seven more, so that's eight altogether."

"Eight, huh?" Brad sounded calmer. "How old is this guy?"

"How should I know? He's my boss. Much older than me, that's all I know."

Owen murmured something.

"I still don't like it," Brad said. "In fact, I've been feeling guilty almost since the day you left. Mom's right, this one went too far. Since you stuck it out about halfway—several weeks longer than I expected, quite frankly—I've decided we can call it a draw and you can come home now."

"You've decided?" she echoed, indignant. "*You've* decided I can come home?"

Owen's low-pitched chuckle tickled her neck.

"Stop that," she hissed.

"Stop what?" asked her brother.

"Stop…trying to boss me around."

"Nice save," acknowledged Owen.

"For God's sake, Liv, grow up. If it makes you feel better we can say *we* decided to end it. Or we can vote. I vote we call off the bet right now."

"I vote you butt out," she shot back. "If you think I've spent all this time suffering and scrimping and barely surviving to give up now, you are very mistaken, Bradford."

Owen lifted his head and cocked one dark brow. "Bradford?"

"Hell, Liv, I was only…"

"Well, don't," she snapped, shooting Owen a warning look as he managed to slide every inch of his naked body over hers in the process of leaving the bed. Ignoring the look, he lingered long enough to kiss her lightly and say, "I'll meet you in the shower."

"What did he say?" Brad demanded.

"He said it's time for the campers to hit the showers. Sometimes they need a little prodding from me to stay on schedule. Thanks for checking on me, Brad. Gotta go. Love you. Call you next week."

"Halfway," she mused after hanging up. Brad was right: she was halfway through her planned stay in Danby. She pressed her lips together. When had she stopped thinking of her time there as a sentence or ordeal and begun looking on it as some sort of adventure? The answer was obvious—it happened when she became involved with Owen.

Regardless of what she called it, the fact remained that she had only a few weeks left to make Owen realize that he loved her as much as she loved him. She was sure he did. He might refuse to say the words, but he told her he loved her over and over throughout the day, in the way he smiled at the sight of her and found excuses to touch her and went out of his way to make her life easier.

And he told her in the way he made love to her, every night, sometimes all through the night. At times the message was hard and fast and reckless, other times it was like floating on a slow-moving river. But always, when they were both sated and their bodies limp, when he was holding her close and she rested her head on his chest, she heard in the frantic pounding of his heart all the things he was afraid to say in words. And that was the message she heard most clearly of all.

Owen turned on the kitchen radio in hopes of catching a weather forecast. Due to several delays that morning, most notably the long shower they'd shared following her brother's wake-up call, it was well past the breakfast hour and he was hungry. He gathered the ingredients for omelets, whistling contentedly as he lined them up on the counter. It occurred to him that he did that a lot lately, whistle contentedly. Hell, he was content. And happy. And Olivia was the reason.

How was it possible for her to transform every moment of every day simply by being there? Being in his life? Everything he thought, everything, came back to Olivia now. Everything he saw, everything he wanted these days was somehow connected to Olivia. He would see something and want to tell her about it, get an idea and want her opinion on it, feel something and get an urge to share it with her.

This wasn't like him. And it wasn't smart. The more he let her into his life now, the harder it was going to be for him to let her go when the time came.

Three weeks. He hadn't marked the day on the calendar. He didn't need to. It was stuck in his head, always hovering right below the level of full consciousness. Possible to avoid, but not to forget. He was well aware he ought to start making the break now, today, cutting back the time he spent with her, extending the time he managed to keep his hands off her. From, say, one hour to two. He knew all the things he *should* be doing. He just didn't want to do them. Not yet. Not as long as there was the tiniest bit of wiggle room.

He could handle having her be part of his daily routine, he assured himself whenever he thought about it. He understood that he would miss her when she was gone, and that for a while he would be lonely and miserable. He'd miss her while he did the things they had done together, like eating breakfast and listening to music or taking the dogs on a walk through the surrounding woods. But eventually he would get over it.

It was much riskier to mess around with emotional stuff. Sharing plans and dreams in any way would sear the time they spent together into his memory indelibly. Worse, it would leave him fighting the same battle on two fronts, one of them inside himself. It was this subtle form of mingling he had to keep in check. He was confident he would know when he was nearing the danger point, when she was about to become so much a part of his world that her leaving would tear it apart. He wasn't sure how he would know, since he'd never come close to sharing anything more significant than dinner and bed with a woman, but he would know. And then he would start winding things down.

"...intermittent showers throughout the day, becoming heavier tonight with high winds and the possibility of some hail." The weatherman cum comedian played a preprogrammed snatch of "Winter Wonderland."

"Yes, folks, it's almost that time again. I'll be back on the hour to update…"

He switched off the radio and turned on the heat under the Teflon coated omelet pan. This was the second rainy Friday in a row. He should be worrying about the outdoor work that needed to be done. Instead he was smiling and thinking it was a good excuse to stay in bed all day. Not that they needed a good one. Even a flimsy one would do. But the rain also provided a legitimate reason for him to insist on driving Olivia to Sugar's again this week. After taking first prize last Friday night, there was no chance she would miss tonight's third and final competition even if it were raining bowling balls.

Recalling her performance last Friday, he smiled in spite of himself. She could sing. And she could act the part of a vamp to perfection…to the unbridled delight of the men in the audience. He had loved watching her move in a close-fitting black vest and slacks, her props a top hat and cane she'd found in one of the antique shops a few miles north of town. He hadn't known about the cane and hat until she walked on stage with them. He also hadn't known that beneath the bulky sweater she removed before taking the stage, she was wearing only a skimpy vest.

What he had not enjoyed was watching other men watching her perform. It was ironic, he'd thought at the time, he'd spent more than half his life avoiding the emotion of jealousy, terrified he would be no better at controlling it than a string of his male ancestors had been. And he'd done an excellent job of it. As a result, he had no notion how much jealousy was *too* much for a man to feel. He was like a first-time driver at the wheel of a high-performance car with its speedometer ripped out. He knew he was moving, and fast, but lacked both the experience and inner signposts to put it in perspective.

All he knew for sure was that a couple of times during her act he'd had a clear vision of himself at the center of a brawl before it was over. Fortunately, it never even came close to that and the person most responsible for keeping things cool was Olivia herself. He had to admit, if only to himself, that when it came to discouraging unwanted attention, she didn't need anyone's help. She had one particular icy glare that got through to even the most booze-drenched admirers. Those less inebriated she merely had to smile at to render them speechless and transfixed. She could look out for herself...and with far more grace and humor than he'd ever manage.

There was still no way she was going there without him.

When the second omelet was ready, he slid it onto a plate, retrieved the one warming in the oven and called for Olivia to come to breakfast. He poured juice and added a plate of toast and still she hadn't appeared.

He found her in the backyard, all four dogs sprawled out around her, harem-style, while she fussed with Jez's collar.

"Hey," he called, crossing the yard. "I thought you said you were hungry enough to eat a horse."

She glanced up and quickly pressed her finger to her lips. "Shh. I think they're really starting to warm to me. I don't want them to get the idea I'd say a thing like that about a fellow member of their animal kingdom."

"You must be very hungry," he pronounced somberly. "It's making you delirious. Come eat before you really lose it and decide to take a *b-i-t-e* out of one of my *d-o-g-s*. Don't worry, they can't spell."

"Very funny. Just let me finish getting this buckled and…there. How's that, Jez?" she crooned. "A little more comfy?"

Jez responded by licking the wrist of the hand Olivia was using to stroke her head.

Intrigued, Owen hunkered down beside her. "What are you doing?"

"I noticed yesterday that she jerked her head a little when I scratched her neck, so I checked her out and found a rough edge on the buckle of her collar. I filed it down with my nail file and I think she's a lot happier. Aren't you, sweetie?" she crooned.

"Thanks, but that wasn't necessary," he said, not sure why his shoulder muscles had tensed up on him. "I hadn't noticed anything out of the ordinary with her, so if you did, you should have let me know."

"You probably didn't notice because you've been busy clearing brush and building walls, while Jez and I have been spending a lot of time together." With a slightly silly grin, she stood and rubbed her palms together briskly. Jez immediately sat up straighter and perked her ears.

"Watch," she said to him. "I sing to her in French and she sings along. Sometimes." She demonstrated, beaming like a proud parent when after she'd sung a half dozen lines, Jez joined in with a whining sound.

"Good girl," she exclaimed, bending down to hug a preening Jez. "I only wish I'd started working with her sooner. Maybe I could have worked her into the act tonight. I think she deserves a reward. Do you have one of those treats in your—" She stopped as soon as she noticed his rigid expression. "You don't mind, do you?"

"Actually, I do," he answered, trying to quell his temper. "These aren't show dogs, Olivia. They work for a living, and the way they work is by doing exactly what I tell them to do. Sometimes the dog's life and mine depend on it. I won't have them responding to commands from anyone else. I thought you understood that."

"I'm sorry, I didn't think what I was doing was the same as giving a command. We were only having a little...fun."

He waited for her temper to kick in, for a verbal slam or colorful comment on what he could do with his orders. But she looked only contrite. And concerned. More genuinely concerned about the consequences of what she had done than he would have thought possible the first day he met her.

Now he felt angry *and* like a jerk.

"No damage done," he told her, attempting to compensate for his gruff tone by forcing a smile. "Let's eat."

Even if it hadn't been the best omelet any man had ever made for her and her turn at dish duty, Olivia still would have insisted on doing the dishes. She could use some time to think, and she'd discovered she did some of her clearest thinking while she was washing dishes. By hand, no less. There was a state-of-the-art dishwasher less than a foot away, but the soothing warm water and mindless repetition of the hands-on approach was more conducive to thinking. Her mouth quirked as she imagined what the reaction would be if she offered to wash dishes when she returned home. *If* she returned home.

That was what she needed to think over. Was she really sure a life in Danby was what she wanted? That was a no-brainer. The answer was no. She wasn't sure, one way or the other. She couldn't even begin to list all the major and minor changes that would be involved, so how could she possibly predict how she'd handle them?

There was, however, one thing of which she was very certain, more certain than she had ever been of anything, and that was that she wanted to spend her life with Owen Rancourt. She wanted to share home and hearth and a bed with him; she wanted a family with him, with all that entailed, babies and car pools and a minivan. She paused in the middle of rinsing a plate. Strike the minivan.

She still wanted the rest. She wanted all the things she had begun to believe she would never want except in romantic daydreams about her future. There were times when she'd wondered if her parents were the exception that proves the rule, and if when it came to finding a mate, normal people ended up "settling" for the best of what they had to choose from. She hated the very idea of settling. She'd promised herself she was going to wait for a man who swept her off her feet even if it took forever. It had begun to look as if it might take that long, until she met Owen.

She couldn't swear under oath that the jolt she'd felt that first day in the diner had been her world grinding to a complete halt so it could instead spin in the opposite direction, but it might as well have been that. The effect on her life had been every bit as profound. Until then, her view of her future had been like the fuzzy image in a funhouse mirror. She still didn't have the details worked out, but she was certain of the one detail that held together all the rest. The one thing she knew absolutely was that Owen was the man she wanted to grow old with.

She grinned, imagining him in twenty years, and thirty, and liking what she saw ahead. If sharing life with Owen meant calling Danby home, so be it. Truthfully, Danby was growing on her. She'd made a few friends and was surprised at how easily she had eased into the unhurried way lives were lived in a small town. More than anything, though, she liked the freedom to make her own first impressions, good or bad, rather than having her name and bank balance and several generations of privilege precede her every place she went. In Danby she was free to be herself all the time, and she was curious to see whom that self would turn out to be.

The role of Olivia Templeton Ashfield had been waiting for her in the delivery room the day she was born. From the start she was a natural for it, and she performed with flawless range and enthusiasm. Now she was ready to do a little improvising. It dawned on her that as much as she claimed—and truly believed—that she always did exactly what she wanted to do, the reality was that she was usually motivated by a desire to prove something, or defy something, or just to avoid something or someone. Maybe herself.

She couldn't change her past or her family history, and she wouldn't even if she could. She was proud of her family, past and present, of their accomplishments and how their generosity kept pace with their success. At the same time she'd always had a restless streak and no idea what to do with it. Now she did, and it was exciting to look ahead and see new and unexpected possibilities.

They were possibilities she might never have encountered if she hadn't been so damn stubborn and refused to crumble when Brad had called her bluff. It would take time, but she would find a place in Danby that was right for her. If not, she'd just have to make one, she decided, tossing aside the dish towel she'd used to dry her hands.

After only a few steps she hesitated and glanced over her shoulder.

"Darn it," she muttered, returning to hang up the towel and deciding she might as well hand dry the dishes and put them away. She enjoyed the feeling of accomplishment that came with finishing a job and stepping back to savor the results. Also, it meant more time to think. With the Danby problem more or less resolved, she was left with only one decision to make. A critical one. What was the best way to go about convincing Owen that he couldn't live without her?

After the dishes, she spent some time with the dogs, tossing Frisbees until her fingers got too cold to hold them. Deciding to look on the bright side, she acknowledged that, thanks to their little prebreakfast tiff, she could rule out at least one approach that would *not* work in her favor, and that was moving in on Owen's turf without being invited. She was pretty sure tossing a Frisbee wasn't crossing that line, but since he'd driven into town to take care of some business matters, including placing a Help Wanted ad in the newspaper, he wouldn't be back anytime soon.

Burying her hands in the fleece-lined pockets of her leather jacket, she jogged down to the cabin she had been staying in to gather together some more of her clothes. Gradually all of her belongings were making their way to the house. She got a little thrill from seeing her toothbrush hanging next to his, her moisturizer standing beside his shaving foam. Domestic intimacy was one more thing she was glad she had waited to share with the man she wanted to give her heart to.

Carrying the clothes she wanted for that night, she'd just closed the cabin door behind her when from the corner of her eye she caught a flash of bright blue off to her left. It must have been something just inside the woods about twenty yards away, she reasoned, seeing nothing now. She watched for a moment or so, but she didn't see anything else out of the ordinary. Probably just some litter carried there on the wind, she decided, shivering enough to get her moving again.

She wondered if the on-and-off drizzle would turn into rain by nightfall. She half hoped it did. Rain had brought her luck last week; perhaps it would do the same tonight. Recalling Owen's long-suffering expression when he grumbled about supposing she'd need a ride again tonight brought a grin to her face. He really was very sweet—chivalrously protective on one hand and, on the other, scared spitless of admitting how much he cared about her.

The news that Danny wouldn't be returning to work had been a disappointment, but Owen agreed he was wise to finish his education. Danny still planned to work summers, but Owen knew he needed more than that. In fact, he told her that losing Danny forced him to do something he'd been putting off for months. He needed to come up with a long-range plan for the camp, and that meant permanent staff.

His business was growing quickly, and it was becoming more difficult all the time to get by with himself, only one full-time employee and hunting for temporary help to get him through the busiest periods. He explained to her that when he started out, his profits had been small and unpredictable, and he hadn't wanted to hire anyone only to let them go if the business hit a rough patch. Instead he handled nearly everything himself and work became his whole life.

It paid off and when it did, he had to work harder than ever. As his reputation spread, there were more requests for him to give workshops and lead training sessions around the country. Then there was the private training, in which handlers who, for whatever reason, were unable to train their dogs, sent them to Owen. During one late-night conversation, he'd revealed to Olivia that it was the private training, working one-on-one with a dog to bring out his full potential, that he loved most. Not only was the process rewarding along the way, but he liked knowing the dog he returned to the handler would work hard, maybe even save a life, and in his view there was nothing better than being even a small part of that. Listening, she had fallen another little bit in love with him.

It was ironic that she understood his feelings so well because, in a way, they resembled her own. She wanted to bring out all the love and intimacy Owen was so determined to keep locked inside him. The more time they spent together, the more aware she was of what he would cringe to hear her refer to as his "sensitive side." Beneath the gruff, macho exterior was a soul that knew how to be gentle and tolerant and forgiving of everyone except himself. And it was making her task one part mystery, one part frustration.

At one point she'd pestered him into naming what he found *least* rewarding about his work, thinking afterward she really shouldn't have needed to ask. The piles of papers and stacks of bills that dotted the otherwise uncluttered house were a dead giveaway. Here lived a man who hated paperwork. And Olivia knew why— because he had to sit still to do it.

She had been teasing when she'd accused him of being a man of action, but it was true. She could hear it in his voice and see it in the excitement in his eyes when he told stories about the searches he'd been called out on. Though the purpose for the search often shook him emotionally, he thrilled to the hunt itself.

It hadn't occurred to her before, but Owen was really a different version of the same male blueprint that had turned out her father and brothers and countless other men who ran the world, or thought they did. Like them, Owen knew what he wanted and how to make it happen. He was a problem solver, a risk taker. He thought on his feet and wasn't afraid to get his hands dirty and could be counted on to see a job through to the end, no matter what. The difference between him and the others was that Owen did it on a...

She hesitated.

Not a smaller scale, she thought, grasping for the right word. There was nothing small about risking your life to save someone you'd never met. As she thought about it more, her heart filled with warmth and she decided she was right the first time. Owen did work on a much smaller scale than most powerful men. About as small as you could get really. The changes he made in the world were accomplished one at a time. It was the way he worked best, she thought, loving him even more...loving him more than she had known she could.

Just like that she was struck by a brilliant idea, a foolproof plan, a reason to feel confident. She wasn't out to make Owen fall in love with her. He already had. And she couldn't change the tragedies he'd endured in the past. All she could do was show him that sharing his life with her would be worth whatever risk he had so thoroughly convinced himself would result.

With that in mind, she recalled his brusque disapproval of her little demonstration with Jez, then she considered the fresh stack of mail he'd tossed on the kitchen counter. Soon he would move it to the table in the hallway and eventually to the overflowing box on the desk in his office. It was obvious to her where her assistance would not be welcome but where it was needed desperately.

Admittedly, she wasn't exactly the bookkeeper type, but she would make a world-class girl Friday. A little of this, a little of that and an occasional zany escapade to keep things interesting...she was a natural. My God, why had it taken her so long to see the light?

She wouldn't go poking around in his private files until she cleared it with him, but she could at least put some kind of order to the mountains of paper. After that she would make a list of all the ways an ambitious girl Friday could make herself indispensable.

Chapter Twelve

Several hours later when Owen arrived home, Olivia was standing at the stove, squinting at the rumpled copy of a recipe in her left hand and stirring the cream sauce with her right. Tucked away in her pocket was the list that had taken longer to draw up than she'd anticipated. The first item on that list was: learn to cook.

The instant he saw her, Owen cursed himself for not going directly to his office at the back of the house as he'd planned to. Instead, stopping just inside the door to wipe his boots and shrug out of his damp jacket, he caught a whiff of something burning and decided he'd better check it out. The smell led him to the kitchen and Olivia. She had flour on her nose and was wearing a loose waist-length sweater that begged him to put his hands underneath. He shoved both hands in his front pockets to keep from reaching out, but there was nothing he could do to slake the hunger erupting full force in his belly at the sight of her. Nothing, that is, except drag her off to bed and make love to her for a week or so. Maybe then his need to have her would burn off and he could get her out of his head. Maybe.

All he knew for certain at that moment was that between the craving to touch her skin and the urge to ravish her right where she stood, the wall of common sense and firm resolutions he'd spent the afternoon reinforcing threatened to crumble once again. One look at her, one brief drift into fantasy, and his plan to keep his distance and cool things down—for both their sakes—was shot straight to hell.

"Hey, there," she greeted, glancing over her shoulder. "Your timing is perfect. There's a fresh pot of coffee there. I'd pour you a cup, but I'm afraid to stop stirring this sauce." Slanting him a self-derisive smile, she added, "This is my second attempt. The first was a disaster."

"Is that what smells?"

She wrinkled her nose and nodded. "I had to disconnect your smoke alarm."

"I'll take care of it," he told her. "Since when do you cook?"

"Since today," she replied brightly. "I hope you like chicken Cordon Bleu, because if all goes well, that's what this could turn out to be."

She lifted the spoon and watched a white glob plop back into the pan.

Her shoulders drooped and her sorrowful expression did something dangerous to his heart.

"Turn the heat to low," he advised.

She followed his suggestion. "Thanks. It's a lot to learn in one day."

Now she was not only tugging at his damn heart, she

was melting it. He smiled in spite of himself. "Yeah. Learning everything there is to know about cooking could take you three, four days, maybe as long as a week."

"I don't mind."

"Why should you? When you get bored, you can just move on to whatever you feel like doing next."

"I suppose," she agreed distractedly, more concerned with what she was doing.

Walk away, walk away, urged his common sense.

Ignoring it, he moved closer to her with the excuse of checking out the contents of the pan.

"What do you think?" she asked.

He thought he should have stayed on the other side of the room where he hadn't noticed the faint sheen this effort had put on her lovely throat and the wisps of hair that had escaped from the knot on top of her head to curve enticingly around her face.

"Olivia, sweetheart, see those big bubbles? That's what's known in the world of cooking as a full boil. Doesn't your recipe say something about removing it from the heat around now?"

"It might," she replied, holding it up to take a look while he reached in front of her and turned off the heat. "It's hard to read the words because the ink ran when I got my hands wet."

Taking the paper from her, he looked at it and shook his head. "Where did you get this?"

"LearnToCook.com. I hope you don't mind that I used your computer?"

"No, not at all." He'd give her the damn computer and everything else he owned—with the possible exception of his dogs—if it would take away one scintilla of the heartache that lay ahead. It wouldn't. Nothing would. His only hope of doing what had to be done was to keep reminding himself that she wasn't the type to pine away over any man, never mind one with nothing to offer but complications and a roll in the hay. She'd figure that out on her own sooner or later. He was simply going to do what he could to make it sooner.

"Do you want to see what else I did today?" she asked, looking excited and very young.

"Sure."

"Follow me." She turned and left the room. He covered the sauce so it wouldn't form a skin and followed her into his office.

"Consider yourself organized," she said, waving her hand with a flourish at the desktop, bare except for the leather-bound blotter he hadn't seen in months and a tray of pens and pencils...freshly sharpened pencils, he noted. On the long table within easy reach of the desk were uniform stacks of manila folders, neatly labeled, and two brand-new file holders that had been gathering dust in a corner since he'd brought them home from the office supply store. They now held hanging folders, and since there wasn't a scrap of paper lying around anywhere, he assumed those files must hold the mass of paperwork he'd been meaning to get around to one of these days.

There was some kind of uncanny magic at work here, he mused. If by some miracle he'd been given the use of an angel for one day, this is the very thing he would wish for her to do. He felt like a kid on the first day of summer, set free from a suffocating burden. That Olivia had made it happen, without him ever saying a word about it, overwhelmed him. It made the backs of his eyes burn in a way they hadn't in a lot of years. And made his blood run cold.

He'd been wrong to think he would know when he was nearing the edge of the cliff in his feelings for Olivia. He was there, over the edge and hanging by only a thread.

He'd been even more wrong to believe he'd had everything he needed in his life. Before Olivia came to him, he'd had nothing. She was everything. It was going to take years for him to get over her. Wrong again, he thought bitterly. It was going to take longer than forever.

He would never be free of her, but she was never going to know. Any hint of the truth would drag out the inevitable.

Beyond the confusing churning in his head, Olivia was delivering a gleeful step-by-step report of the miracle she had performed on his behalf. Owen nodded and smiled and pretended to listen.

What in God's name was he going to do about this? About her? He couldn't come right out and order her back to her own bed. But how could he go on living under the same roof, sleeping in the same bed and making love over and over to the one woman who was the answer to every prayer he had been afraid to pray, and not surrender everything to her? Everything he was? Everything he would ever be?

He couldn't. It was that simple. And that complicated.

"I even color-coded your scheduling calendar," she told him, holding it up for him to see.

Owen blinked and focused on it. Then on her. "Why?"

"So you can see at a glance how many lectures you have scheduled for that month, how many private sessions, when you..."

He cut her off. "I meant, why did you move all my stuff around without checking with me?"

"I wanted to surprise you," she answered, wariness just starting to edge aside the delight in her voice and turn her eyes a stormy blue. "I didn't look at anything or open any envelopes, if that's what's worrying you. All I did was sort everything into broad categories and made a place for each category." Folding her arms in front of her, she looked at him with slightly narrowed eyes. "Frankly, I expected you to be grateful."

"For what? You messing everything up so it'll probably take me an hour every time I need to put my hand on something?"

"No, for digging you out of the mess you were already in. And as for 'putting your hand on something,' you can read, can't you?" She snatched up one of the folders and held it right in front of his face. "See? I even printed the words in big letters to make it easier for you."

"You did, huh? Well, I've got news for you, *cupcake,* nothing you've done makes my life easier. Not mixing up my mail or sticking colored dots on my schedule or screwing around with the dogs I've spent years training…and not burning something and stinking up the kitchen so you can indulge your sudden impulse to cook."

"What are you talking about?"

"You," he said bluntly. "You and your expensive, pampered life. I'm talking about your *real* life, not a few weeks of slumming to amuse yourself or break the monotony."

"What the hell do you know about my life? Real or otherwise?"

"Only what you've told me, sweetheart. I sure don't

have any firsthand knowledge of a life that's just one whim after another. You said it better than I ever could; you do what you want, when you want. You want to move to Danby, you move to Danby. You want to throw a pot of hot coffee at someone, you throw it. You want to let some guy screw your brains out, you do it.''

Pain and anger flashed and warred in her eyes. ''Is that what you think it was? A whim? Do you think you're just *some guy?*''

''I know it. I was what you wanted at that moment. Your words, cupcake.''

''Don't call me that. Don't you ever call me that again. You're mocking me…and you're twisting my words to suit you.''

''I'm not twisting anything. I'm just telling the truth.''

''Why? Why now? Because I moved around some papers? Because I played with one of your dogs? That's so lame it's laughable.''

''Feel free to laugh. It won't change the facts.''

''It won't, huh? Well, then, I will. Fact one, you don't like my colored dots…'' She picked up the nearest file holder and flipped it so files scattered across the floor. Owen refrained from comment as she did the same with the second, then cleared the top of both the table and desk with a sweep of her arm. When she spun to face him, her expression was a red-hot blaze of triumph. ''There. All back the way it was, only a little lower, that's all. Let's see…''

He followed as she stalked to the kitchen. ''My cooking stinks?'' She hauled the trash container from the cupboard beneath the sink and quickly dumped the dinner she'd made for him, including the cream sauce. ''Problem solved. And you have my word I will never again sing in the presence of your dogs.'' Her brows furrowed, as she appeared to be thinking hard. ''I'm just not quite sure how to go about unscrewing brains, but just as soon as I figure it out, I'll let you know.''

''Now who's being ridiculous?''

''I guess I am,'' she retorted. ''But don't worry, it's only a whim. In a minute I'll be on to something else.''

''Olivia, there's no sense in getting all worked up over this.''

''Over what?'' she demanded loudly. ''I'm not even sure what this is about because it's sure as hell not about colored dots.''

''You're right. And I'm sorry. You obviously worked hard and thought you were helping. I shouldn't have said what I did. I wouldn't have if I hadn't been already on edge when I walked in.''

''About what?'' she asked, her face softening as she stepped closer.

Owen gritted his teeth and sidestepped her.

''I knew something was bothering you. You can talk about it with me, Owen,'' she told him, her tone gentle. ''You can always talk to me. About anything.''

''Okay.'' Averting her eyes, he swung a kitchen chair around and straddled it. ''I did a lot of thinking today and the more I thought about it, the more I realized this isn't working.''

''You mean us. We're not working.'' Olivia paused while he confirmed her statements with a nod. Her chin came up a notch. ''Now that is strange, because everything seemed to be working just fine this morning.''

''In bed, you mean. Sure, we get along just fine between the sheets,'' he agreed, his gritty tone aloof, his choice of words intentional, meant to shatter any romantic illusions she might be harboring about him.

"I'm a man, you're a woman. That's half the battle right there."

"I see."

"That'll burn itself out in a while."

"We'll see, won't we?" she countered, her disbelief in full view.

"Actually we won't. That's what I'm getting at," he said, and watched her breathing catch. "I'd rather quit while we're ahead. What's that saying you show-biz types have? Something like 'always leave 'em wanting more.' I think that's what we should do. I'm pretty sure your room is still available in town."

"Are you throwing me out?" she inquired, her tone reserved and difficult to read.

"Of course not. I just think it would make it easier all the way around if you moved back to town. You know there's nothing left to do that you can handle."

"I see. What about our deal?"

"Deal?" He struggled to remember. "Oh, you mean agreeing that you'd stay until Danny came back to work."

"Right. Our deal. The one we shook on."

"I'd say it doesn't apply since Danny's not coming back."

"Of course he's coming back," she argued.

"Not until next summer." He looked at her eloquently raised brows. "Don't be ridiculous."

"I'm not. At least, not as ridiculous as a grown man so scared of me he'd rather pick a fight than face the truth. The real truth. Not those supposed facts of yours."

"I'm not picking a fight."

"That's exactly what you're doing."

"And I'm certainly not scared of you." He managed

an amused chuckle. "Now we're really talking laughable."

"Really? I don't think so. I think we're talking shaking-in-your-boots scared. Let's find out who's right." Two unhurried steps brought her against the back of the chair he was straddling. She grabbed the front of his shirt with fisted hands. Tugged. "Kiss me, Owen."

He stared up at her cool eyes and the reckless challenge of her mouth and tried to breathe normally in spite of feeling as though his lungs had sealed shut.

She tugged on his shirt again, harder. "Stand up and kiss me and tell me if what you feel for me is something that's close to burning out, or something that scares the hell out of you. Just one kiss and then you can toss me out of here on my butt."

His heart was pounding hard enough to throw off sparks. The need ripping him apart was primal, violent. He couldn't think. But some things he knew without thinking. He knew he couldn't kiss her and make her go. He couldn't *not* kiss her and survive.

He was on his feet, the chair between them and his hands already moving through her hair. The knot loosened and then came undone, and her long, silky hair fell across his face as his mouth locked onto hers. It was him coming undone then, sliding all the way back to that morning as if the time since didn't exist, as if he hadn't made up his mind not to do this, as if no decisions had been made, no lies spoken.

He kicked the chair away and jerked her closer. Her tongue swirled and danced with his; her hands tugged his shirt from his jeans and slipped inside. She touched his skin and they were melded together, sharing breath and heat and desire.

When the phone rang, he ignored it. When it stopped,

he moved his mouth to her throat and his hands to her breasts. When it rang again, the part of him that never shut off, his sense of responsibility, took over.

He lifted his head, heard her moan and kept one arm around her as he reached for the phone. "Yeah?"

Olivia rested her head on his chest, loving the solid feel of him, the strength and reassuring substance of his body that made simply being near him a heady pleasure. When he took his arm away and moved to the far end of the counter where he kept a pen and notepad, she wanted to cry or stamp her foot. She did neither and was glad she resisted the urge when his side of the phone conversation revealed that he was being asked to join in a search for someone. She stood silently as he jotted down some information.

"Give me twenty minutes," he said. He turned to hang up the phone, and his gaze collided with hers. He blinked as though he'd forgotten she was there. His expression was all business, and Olivia understood that everything else had to be put on hold until he did what he'd been called out to do.

He righted the chair and kept his hands firmly on the back of it. "Look, I'm sorry."

"Don't be. I understand completely. Is someone lost?"

He nodded. "A kid. A boy. Eight years old. He's from out of state, up here with his grandparents to see the foliage." He opened the closet door and pulled out a leather harness she'd never seen before. "He's been missing for hours, the sky's about to break open and they just now decide it might be a good idea to use dogs."

"Are you taking all four of them?" she asked.

"No. Only Radar. I've got a feeling the weather's

going to get a lot worse before the night's over, and I'm not having Romeo out in that when he's still not feeling 100 percent.''

"Of course not.''

She felt useless and restless, looking on while he moved around efficiently, filling a thermos with hot coffee and his pockets with small pieces of beef jerky, and finally putting on a long, heavy jacket that was also unfamiliar to her. Like the jacket and harness, this was a side of him she'd known was there but had never seen.

He paused at the kitchen door and took out his wallet. "I'm sorry I have to rush off in the middle of this...though it might be better this way. We'll talk again,'' he said in a tone that tried hard to be friendly and reassuring. "But for now, this should more than cover whatever wages I owe you.''

He laid a stack of fifties on the table. Olivia felt her entire body freeze, then start to heat. If he noticed her grinding her teeth, he didn't show it.

"I'll be gone a couple of hours, anyway. Maybe all night. I'm asking you to make it easier on both of us and be gone when I get back.''

Chapter Thirteen

It was dusk when he left. Olivia saw him lead an already-excited Radar to the truck and drive away, watching until the red specks of his taillights disappeared.

She pressed a kiss to the glass with her fingertips and whispered again what she'd said as he walked out the door. "Be careful. I love you."

He'd said nothing in return.

After he was gone, she sat and looked at the darkness outside deepen and tried to keep the same from happening in her heart. It was hard not to feel deflated. She'd been picturing tonight in her mind all afternoon. Except, in that picture, she was not sitting alone, feeling empty and dazed, the way a fighter feels when he's taken too many hits to the head. Punch-drunk, that's what they called it. She felt punch-drunk, only the hits she'd taken were to the heart.

It helped, a little, to know that Owen had not wanted

to hurt her. Oh, he knew very well that's what he was doing. But picking a fight with her had been as much a part of his calculated plan as cooking dinner had been part of hers. She almost smiled, thinking that if they ever set their sights on the same goal, they'd be unstoppable.

It didn't help at all to recall the regret and sadness haunting his eyes as he told her how little their time together meant to him. Not because she believed a bit of it, but because she knew it had hurt him to do what he was convinced he had to do to protect her. And it hurt her to see him hurting, because she loved him. Oh, what a tangled web, she thought. Who'd have guessed that love could be every bit as convoluted as a lie?

And the money. She glanced at the pile of bills still on the table and shook her head. If it weren't so silly, she would be offended. "This will more than cover whatever wages I owe you," she mimicked. If he hadn't been in such a hurry, and for such a good reason, she would have asked what he was paying her for…shoveling dirt or sharing his bed. But then, if the phone hadn't rung when it did, she wouldn't have had to ask. The way he was kissing her at that moment did not suggest he was in a mood to throw her out.

She wouldn't have gone, anyway. No more than she intended to leave now. Owen couldn't have been more right about one thing. She did usually get what she wanted. And she wanted him, badly, but only if he was able to admit he wanted her the same way. She would never beg a man to love her, not even the man she loved so much it felt as if in a small corner of her heart she had always known him and had waited for him, only him, all the time she'd thought she was simply waiting.

No, she wouldn't beg him. But she also wasn't about

to give up without more of a fight than that little skirmish tonight. Still, as stubborn as she was, she knew better than to go head to head with Owen in a war of wills. Instead she would rely on the ladylike art of serenity, otherwise known as patience. She'd waited out destiny, and she could surely wait out one thickheaded man.

If she did eventually decide to pick up the mess in his office and clean up the kitchen, she wasn't at that point yet. Instead she chose a mystery from his bookcase and curled up on the sofa to read, or at least distract herself from wondering and worrying about how the search was going. She was worried, darn it, and nervous, and when the phone rang, she jumped a good five inches off the sofa.

She hurried to the kitchen to answer and immediately recognized Brad's voice. They exchanged basic pleasantries and then she asked why he was calling.

"Can't I call just to say hello to my little sister and see how she's doing?"

"No," Olivia retorted. "The deal is I call you to check in. Remember?"

"I do now." He sighed audibly. "I guess I'll have to forfeit."

"I decline the offer. But nice try."

"I taught you too well," he groused.

"You'd like to think so, I'm sure. Now what do you really want?"

"Where's your boss tonight?" he asked casually, instead of answering the question.

"He got called away on his other job."

"What's his other job?"

"It's a long story," she told him.

"Too long for long distance?"

"Much."

"In that case, fix your face and I'll swing by to take you to dinner...assuming there's a restaurant in Danby."

"There are several. Unfortunately, none of them will be open by the time you get here. And I'm booked for breakfast," she added to cut him off at the pass.

"What if I'm there in an hour? Will they be closed then?"

"If you're here in an hour, *I'll* buy *you* dinner."

"You're on. Did I mention I'm in Albany?"

"Albany, New York?" she demanded.

"That would be the one," replied Brad, not bothering to hide his insufferably smug chuckle.

Irritated, Olivia tapped her foot and damned herself for being reeled in so easily. It never would have happened if she hadn't been under duress, but she wasn't about to tell that to Brad and be bombarded by more of his nosy questions.

"What are you doing in Albany?"

"I had some business up here and I figured that since I was in your neck of the woods...that is how you country folks refer to it, isn't it?"

"Don't get cute," she warned.

"Don't get touchy. I had business in Albany and wanted to touch base."

"Business, my foot."

He just laughed.

"Brad, all kidding aside, this isn't a good night to come here."

"I won't stay long," he promised.

"You won't stay at all, because you can't come."

"Save your breath, Liv. I'll be there in an hour."

"I won't give you directions, and you'll never find this place on your own."

He chuckled. "Won't I?"

"No," she snapped, not all that sure she was right about that. Brad was nothing if not resourceful. And devious.

"Then you don't have anything to worry about. See you in a while."

"Brad? Brad? Damn you."

She slammed down the phone and screamed through her clenched teeth. She shouldn't be surprised at him pulling a stunt like this. He was as impossible as ever. And when he wasn't being impossible, he was simply annoying.

Exasperated, she flicked the pencil with her finger and sent it rolling across the counter. Maybe she'd luck out and Brad would get lost. And she wouldn't send a search party to look for him, either. At least not for a few days.

Even if he did show up, she might be able to satisfy his curiosity and send him on his way before Owen got home. She expected Owen to come back cold and tired and hungry, and surprised to find her still there. Not necessarily in that order. She would prefer to keep it a private moment. In fact, the less Brad knew about her life there the better, until she was ready to tell her whole family.

With a sigh she pushed away from the counter she'd been leaning against, knocking the small spiral-bound notepad to the floor. She glanced at it as she picked it up. As soon as she read the first line she knew Owen had gone off without the notes he'd jotted down when he was on the phone. Did he need them? she wondered, taking a closer look at what he'd scribbled. His penmanship was abominable, but then she already knew that from trying to decipher her way through his office clutter. She could make out about every other word and guess at a few more. None of it seemed like critical information he couldn't get from someone on the scene. It was pretty much what he'd already told her, with a brief description of the missing boy. He was just over three feet tall, with straight, sandy-colored hair, freckles and a big smile. Definitely a grandparent's description, she thought, feeling only sympathy for the couple who were no doubt blaming themselves.

She almost gave up on the last line. Owen had been running out of room and scrunched his letters together even more than usual. She first thought it read ''loyal bee picnic,'' which made no sense at all. Studying it more, and turning the paper to view it from different angles, she was able to get the first and last words. Royal and parka. Royal bee parka. Royal bee. Her chest tightened. Royal blue. Of course, royal-blue parka. The boy was wearing a royal-blue parka, the same color she'd thought she'd seen through the trees earlier that day.

It could not be a coincidence. Why hadn't she bothered to walk over and check to see if there actually was something—or someone—there? Because she'd been cold and carrying an armful of clothes and had other things on her mind. And now a little boy was wandering around in the woods, cold, wet, no doubt scared…and it would soon get worse, judging by how loud the wind had gotten since Owen left.

She had to do something. She had to tell Owen what she'd seen and let him plan his search accordingly. Otherwise it could be hours, or tomorrow, by the time they got to this area. She decided to call the state police, knowing they would be able to get a message to Owen faster than she could.

She picked up the phone, frowning when she couldn't get a dial tone. Maybe Brad hadn't hung up on her after all. It looked as if the problem was with the phone. More than likely the wind and broken branches were downing telephone lines. The sudden flicker of the lights warned that the power could be the next to go.

She grabbed her jacket and purse, fishing in it for her keys as she ran to her car. It wasn't exactly a shock that the car refused to start, but it did make her want to bang her head on the steering wheel and cry from frustration. Unfortunately, there wasn't time.

She was not a particularly brave woman. She was especially not brave in the woods, alone, at night. The howling wind only made it more frightening, and she didn't even want to consider the possibility of thunder and lightning and dodging falling tree limbs. Only one thing was more unthinkable to her than going into those woods by herself, and that was to go back inside where it was safe and warm, knowing a kid was out there alone. For all she knew the little boy could be just on the other side of that stretch of trees, wandering in circles, or hurt, lying out there alone with a broken leg. Somebody had to check it out, and it looked as if it was going to be her.

It was one of those rare nights when, if he'd had even a scrap less faith, Owen would have believed that God and the elements were conspiring against them. The weather had been lousy when he'd left home and it had only gotten worse since then. No moon, no stars, just the steady rainfall and the wind. The damn wind was the worst of it. It stung your face and had a near-mystical ability to shift directions every time the dogs locked onto a trace of airborne scent, swirling it away and leaving the dogs with their noses up, running in circles. As a rule, track scent was more reliable, but tonight the mud was playing tricks there, as well. On a night like this you were thankful for whatever your dog could get.

Outside the fire station the group, comprised of police and a couple of dozen volunteers, only a few with dogs, had wasted no time dividing up territory and moving out. Anyone willing to do this did it with everything they had in them, every time out. Even so, when the search was for a child, they all dug in a little deeper, stuck it out a little longer and prayed.

He'd hung back when the others started off, wanting a little quiet when he let Radar get the scent off an unwashed baseball jersey belonging to the lost boy. Radar was already shivering with excitement and pawing the ground, but Owen refused to rush, wanting to be sure the dog had the scent before they set off. Not for the first time his throat went dry when he opened the plastic bag with the jersey in it and realized just how small it and the boy were. It made him even more determined to find what he was out there looking for.

For the first mile or so they worked across an open field. Radar wheeled and swerved, cutting back and forth through weeds and scrub grass in search of the boy's scent. When the field ended, heavy brush began. Owen groaned inwardly, but Radar didn't hesitate before charging into it.

All the big dog cared about now was finding a trace of that scent and following it to the source. He didn't worry about foxholes or hanging branches or gnarled tree roots as treacherous as traps. Owen worried about them and a lot more, but he couldn't hold Radar back and expect him to do his job at the same time. The best he could do was constantly look ahead for potential hazards and pull Radar back if he had time. It wasn't easy. On a night like this it was damn near impossible. That's why an hour and a half after they started, he and Radar were back in the truck, heading home.

He'd cringed when he heard the dog's high-pitched yelp of pain, but he'd been only patient and gentle as he crouched beside him in the rain and worked to free his right front paw from the web of wet, leathery tree roots that had brought him down. When he had him back on his feet, Radar kept that paw in the air and attempted to keep going on the other three. It was then that Owen had lifted him into his arms and carried him all the way back to the truck.

Now he had to decide which dog would take the bloodhound's place. As if knowing that, Radar hung his head all the way back. He could really use Romeo tonight, thought Owen, but now that he'd been out himself, he was more resolved than ever that it was too soon to run him that hard. That left Mac and Jez. Both were solid trackers, even in bad weather, but Jez was more high-strung and would take more handling if the storm hanging overhead ripped open. The last thing he needed was an extra challenge. That left Mac.

As soon as the house came into view, thoughts he'd been stoically holding at bay reared up and took command of his brain. Olivia's car was still there. That meant she was, too. He tried to feel angry, or at least annoyed, but it was useless. He was only relieved. That didn't mean he'd changed his mind or lost his resolve, he told himself. He just didn't want her out driving around on a night like this.

He went straight to the house, carrying Radar because it was faster. Inside he was champing at the bit to get back to the search. But first he wanted, he *needed,* to see Olivia. And he didn't want to think about why.

Even before he called her name and got no answer Owen knew she wasn't there. He'd somehow sensed it as soon as he'd walked in the house. More accurately, he'd sensed something missing. He'd done a quick search of all the rooms before thinking to look for a note and finding it propped against the coffeemaker.

He read quickly, his hand starting to tremble after the first few lines.

"What the hell?" he ground out when he'd finished reading. He grasped his head with both hands, mostly to stop it from exploding. What was she thinking of? He closed his eyes, breathing heavily. The boy, obviously. She was thinking of the boy and doing the only thing she could to help him. Now she was out there alone, except for Jez, skittish, high-strung Jez. He'd just heard the first low rumble of thunder, and he was standing there with his heart squeezing out beats, muttering to himself and wasting time.

Leaving Radar inside, he went out the back way, taking with him a dry harness, and a plastic bag containing something that felt like silk and smelled like flowers and sunshine, like Olivia. Grim-faced, he slipped the leather harness onto Romeo. Mac wouldn't do. He needed the strongest dog possible. He'd risked his own life dozens of times, on searches or just because he'd been young and it seemed the right thing to do at the time. But he had never once risked one of his dogs. His loyalty to them was sacrosanct. He would not be violating it and risking Romeo now for anything or anyone but Olivia.

He didn't want to think about what that meant, either. He only wanted to find her and bring her home.

"*L* my name is Linda, my friend's name is Luke, we come from Louisiana and we sell...L'oreal."

"I never heard of Lorell."

"L'oreal," corrected Olivia. "They make cosmetics."

"What..."

"Makeup. Mascara. Lipstick, there, that's an *L*. You must have heard of lipstick?"

"Okay. *M. M* my name is Matt, my friends name is Martha—she's not really my friend though."

"I know, Johnny, I know." The kid issued the same disclaimer every time he was forced to use a girl's name.

He continued with the game, and Olivia continued to divide her attention between playing along and praying harder than she'd ever prayed in her life. She had not found Johnny as close to the house as she would have liked, but she was infinitely grateful the boy had had the sense not to start up into the foothills. He'd been smart enough to hunker down and wait for somebody to find him.

Johnny—or rather Jonathan Kirby Sanders, 107 Applewood Drive, Rockport, Massachusetts, as he had identified himself to Olivia, following to the letter his mother's instructions for what to do if he ever got lost—was a very sensible kid. He had picked up one of the tarps she and Owen had forgotten outside and that had been carried off by the wind, and he knew enough to roll it into a ball and take it with him. When he became too tired to walk and frightened by the noises he heard in the dark, he had found a spot out of the wind and used the tarp as a makeshift shelter.

It was the tarp Olivia saw first as she ran her flashlight back and forth across the "path" Jez was pulling her along. She still wasn't sure who'd been the most excited when they reached him, Johnny, Jez or herself. Johnny went from happy to overjoyed—as overjoyed as a tired, wet, scared kid can be—when she poured him a cup of hot chocolate from the thermos in her backpack and offered him his choice of cheese or chocolate.

He ate most of both, cautiously sharing some with Jez, who had commandeered the spot between them. While they ate, Olivia did what she could to secure the tarp. Having the advantage of height, she was able to reach higher and more sturdy branches. After that, she pulled the blanket she'd brought over the three of them, with Jez's head sticking out between their feet, and they settled in to wait. And play every word game Olivia could remember from childhood.

It wasn't until the thunder started that Jez began to tremble. Olivia tried to calm her with stroking and a steady, reassuring monologue, but she could sense the increasing tension in Jez's powerful muscles. When a violent streak of lightning crackled directly over them, she expected the dog to bolt. She didn't, though her ears remained stiff and her head up, as if she were on high alert. The worst of the storm seemed to have passed and only the howl of the wind broke the vast black silence when Jez shot from under the blanket and took off at a full gallop, ignoring Olivia's frantic calls for her to come back.

Giving up, she took a deep breath, not wanting Johnny to know that she was considerably more frightened with Jez gone.

''Where's she going?'' he asked.

Who knows? thought Olivia. Home, to chase a rabbit, stretch her legs.

''She's gone to look for help,'' she told him. ''You know the search party I told you about? Well, Jez is going to tell them to hurry up and get here.''

''Like Lassie?'' Johnny asked, his hopeful innocence rousing a new, fierce protectiveness in her.

''Right,'' she said brightly, scooting closer and putting her arm around his narrow shoulders. ''Just like Lassie.''

Chapter Fourteen

Maybe Romeo had picked up on Owen's own desperation. More likely the big shepherd made the connection between the scrap of lingerie he'd been given to sniff and the woman it belonged to. If Owen were able to smile, he would have, thinking that he would have to remember to tell Olivia he was absolutely certain Romeo did not hold "the bee thing" against her. Like the man at the other end of his lead, he was working with even more energy and focus than usual. And with no sign he was hurting or off his game, for which Owen was very thankful. It would torment him to have to run the dog hurt, but right now Romeo was his best shot at finding Olivia, and nothing mattered more than that.

He would find her. It was a miserable night and parts of the terrain they were covering were uneven and challenging even in daylight. But the temperature wasn't below freezing and they weren't picking their way up the rocky side of a mountain. Plus the track was fresh. They knew where it originated, and what were now primary scents—Olivia's and Jez's—were familiar to Romeo. All that made this far from the difficult search it might have been had he been looking for anyone else.

He was always the detached professional: immune from the raw emotional freefall loved ones experienced at times like this. He had no experience with this kind of fear, but he was learning one thing fast—it didn't matter where or how far or how cold. When it was someone you loved who was missing, the terrain and fear were infinite.

He would find her. Maybe even before the rest of the searchers, whom he'd radioed to get over here, showed up. He would find her, but right then it felt like a piece of his heart, the biggest piece, was somewhere out there in all that cold, wet darkness.

Owen half believed that the lead connecting him to Romeo was a low-tech form of fiber optic cable because of the way it transmitted information. He relied on those transmissions, always alert to the vibration he felt along his hand and arm when Romeo decided they were getting close.

He felt it now, and reminded himself it was more important than ever that he stay calm and in control, ready to handle whatever injuries or other complications were waiting at the end of the track. *Please, God, let Olivia and the boy be all right, and close.* He'd hardly finished the silent prayer when Romeo shot straight ahead and the beam from his flashlight caught movement from that direction. Jez.

He managed to keep his cool long enough for the two dogs to go through their mutual sniffing ritual and to praise them both. Then he attached to Jez's collar the spare lead he was never without on a search.

"Find, Romeo," he commanded. "Find, Jez, find."

The two dogs plunged ahead, vying for lead position with Romeo invariably winning. The worried man in him wanted to start shouting her name. The tracker in him overrode the fear and kept his mouth shut and put his complete trust in the ultrasensitive noses leading the way.

It took ten minutes, and felt like ten years, till the dogs started barking excitedly. They were close, very close, or they wouldn't lift their noses far enough off the ground to bark. Finally, in between the barks, he heard a voice, Olivia's voice, calling his name. And allowing him to draw his first breath that didn't make his chest ache since learning she was gone.

Owen saw the tarp and then the two figures in front of it, one tall, one not, both waving their arms wildly and shouting. He wanted to run straight to her and wrap his arms around her and assure himself that she was all right. He managed not to, settling instead for a fast, desperate hug, before including the boy, Johnny, in his questions and getting answers from both of them at the same time, their sentences colliding and overlapping, with one starting and the other finishing the same thought until Owen understood hardly anything they were saying and didn't much care. It was enough, all he needed, all he would ever need, he realized, to know that she was there, and unhurt…that is, except for scrapes and scratches on her exposed skin and aches and pains everywhere else.

"I knew you would find us," she told him, squeezing his hand and Johnny's at the same time. "I just didn't think it would be this soon. I figured it would be hours before the search spread this far.''

Owen explained about Radar's accident and how that brought him home to find her note.

''I wanted to strangle you when I read it,'' he told her, unable to stop his gaze from moving over her, making sure again and again that even the smallest part of her was all right. ''I kept asking myself what kind of woman would go running off into the woods on a night like this.''

''You don't have to say it,'' she said with a sigh, her soft pout sheepish. ''A very stupid woman.''

''Wrong,'' he said, indulging his longing to hold her against him just for a moment, ''A brave woman. And a smart one. And the woman I want—''

''Mister, your dog is peeing on a tree.''

Well, that was one way a man could tell his timing was bad. Reluctantly letting Olivia go, he gave Johnny's head a rub. ''Of course he is. Doesn't your mother always tell you to go to the bathroom before you go on a trip?''

''Yes. But your dog isn't going on a trip.''

''Sure he is,'' said Owen, gathering up the blanket and backpack and the other things Olivia had thought to bring. A very smart woman. ''We're all going on a trip.''

''Where to?'' Johnny asked, looking uncertain.

Owen let his eyes meet Olivia's for only a second. ''Home,'' he said. ''We're all going home. But first we have to get you checked out and make sure you're not hiding any broken bones or cauliflower ears, anything like that.''

The boy giggled, but he looked beat. Beyond beat.

Owen quickly wrapped the things he'd picked up in the tarp and shoved it in a vee in a large oak tree.

"I'll get it tomorrow," he told Olivia as he hunkered down with his back to Johnny. "Looks like you could use a lift, Johnny. Climb aboard."

He did, with Olivia's help.

"Are you going to carry me all the way to my house?"

"Not quite," he grunted, straightening. "The doctor has to check you out first. How'd you like to go for a ride in an ambulance with all the lights flashing?"

There was a lot more than an ambulance waiting when they got back to the house. Cars filled the driveway and continued down the drive as far as Olivia could see. The story of Johnny's rescue had already spread through the crowd gathered on the porch and front lawn. It had been relayed to them by whomever Owen had radioed with the news that they were safe and uninjured and heading back.

The crowd cheered and applauded their arrival. Olivia was surprised and embarrassed to find herself being hailed as a hero, receiving a tearful, effusive thank-you from Johnny's grandparents and pats on the back from anyone who got close enough. There was food, pizza and donuts, and someone held aloft T-bones for the dogs, which brought more cheering.

What was anticipated to be a long, nerve-racking night had turned into a celebration. Owen opened the house and people flowed inside. Noting her perplexed expression, he explained that the festive mood was fueled by all the adrenaline that had been short-circuited and needed to be burned off somehow.

"How long will they stay?" she asked.

His mouth curved into a gentle smile. "Tired?"

"A little."

"Liar."

"A lot. You?"

He shook his head, his eyes moving over her face the same slow, deliberate way they had right after he found them. "I'm so relieved there isn't room for anything else." He swallowed hard enough to work his throat muscles and put his hands on her shoulders. "Olivia, I…"

"There you are." She recognized the man standing beside them as one of the firefighters who'd taken part in the search. "Johnny won't let the ambulance take off until he says goodbye to you two."

"Of course," said Olivia, aware of the flicker of annoyance in Owen's eyes as he took his hands off her. It was strange that all of a sudden she was having no difficulty at all reading the look in his eyes. Familiarity, she wondered. Or something else?

She kissed Johnny on the cheek and promised she would see him again before he left Danby. Owen climbed into the back of the ambulance to shake his hand, leaning closer to listen to whatever Johnny had to say.

"You two must have bonded big-time during that piggyback ride," she remarked, watching as the emergency techs helped Johnny's grandmother sign some forms. "He had a lot more to say to you than me, the woman who played 'I Spy' with him."

"Jealous?" he teased, his arm coming around her shoulders.

"Curious."

"He told me you said he could come and visit all the dogs if it was okay with his grandparents."

"I did it to keep his spirits up while we were out there waiting for you to find us."

"You mean waiting for *someone* to find you."

Olivia turned her head and looked up at him. "No. I knew it would be you. I hate to admit it, but that's what finally pushed me into going to look for him. I knew I would be all right in the end because you would come for me. And you did."

"Yeah. I did." He brushed her cheek with the side of his thumb, and she leaned into the caress.

"So is it okay if he visits the dogs?"

"Of course, it's fine."

"Don't worry, I'll make sure no one sings to them."

"Not that tired after all, I see."

She shrugged offhandedly. "What can I tell you? It's a reflex action. I could probably fire back in my sleep."

"There's something to look forward to," he remarked, also offhanded. "Want to know what else the kid told me?"

She nodded.

"He said you smell good."

"Really? That's adorable."

Her pleased smile was still forming when he added, "Radar didn't say so in so many words, but I think he had the same reaction to the white lace thing I gave him to scent off."

Puzzled, she tilted her head to look at him. "What white—" Her eyes widened, and then narrowed. "My camisole? You let him sniff my camisole?"

"If that's what it's called, yes, I did. But only after I checked to make sure it really smelled like you."

"How dedicated of you," she drawled.

"All in the line of duty," he countered. "And you know what, Olivia?"

"I'm not sure I want to."

"The kid was right. You do smell good."

This was a perfect moment, thought Olivia. She was exhausted, wet and dirty, leaning on a man who was even wetter and dirtier, and who only hours ago had paid her for services rendered and told her to get out. It was still a perfect moment. She felt almost as if they were cocooned inside these sixty seconds of happiness. She wanted to believe that Owen had changed his mind about making her leave. If he hadn't, she didn't want to know now. Not yet. She wanted to remain inside this perfect moment with him as long as possible.

At last the ambulance doors were closed, its engine started. "I think it's a good idea for Johnny to spend tonight in the hospital," she commented. "Just in case."

"I'm glad to hear that," said Owen. "It means you'll understand why I radioed ahead for two ambulances."

As he said it, the first of those two ambulances pulled away, revealing the second parked directly behind it.

"Don't talk to me," warned Olivia. "Not one word."

"I haven't said one word since the nurse let me back in here."

"Well then, don't look at me, either."

"Sorry, cupcake, that's beyond my control. Maybe, just maybe, mind you, if you'd gone with the hospital gown, I could look without drooling. But once you made me go fetch this—" he slipped one finger under the strap of her apricot nightgown "—my fate was sealed."

She was almost disgruntled enough to tell him not to

touch her, either. Almost, but not quite. She was enjoying the tantalizing abrasion of his calloused fingertip, enjoying it even more when a second finger found its way beneath her strap. Instead she fell back to grumbling about being tossed in the back of an ambulance and carted away.

"I still don't see why I'm in the hospital. I wasn't lost." She shrugged off the eloquent arch of his eyebrow. "Not in the usual sense. I was a searcher. Like you. How come you're not lying in this bed?"

He had all four fingers inside the strap now, and was edging lower, bit by tingling bit. His voice was husky, and pitched excitingly low, caressing her in a different way. "Is that an invitation, Olivia?"

"If it is, you damn well better refuse it," said a smoother and very hostile voice. "Politely."

She hadn't heard the door open, but it must have, because there was Brad, as large as life and with murder in the hard gaze he had fixed on Owen.

"Did it ever occur to you to knock?" she asked him.

"Yes, and it's a good thing I decided against it." He still didn't take his eyes off Owen, who was looking back with deceptively calm disdain. "Get your hand off my sister, and then get it, and the rest of you, out of this room."

Owen had not yet moved a muscle, and he didn't then.

"Did you hear me?" Brad demanded, not happy being ignored.

"I heard you."

"Then what are you waiting for?"

Owen didn't answer for a few seconds, giving Olivia a bad feeling about where this clash of testosterone was headed.

"Is this really necessary?" she asked.

Neither man so much as glanced her way. It was hard to be heard through all that swollen ego. Her guess was Brad would crack first, but knowing her brother's attitude toward defeat, it was bound to get pretty ugly along the way.

"An introduction," Owen said at last, taking both her and Brad by surprise. "I'm waiting for an introduction. Otherwise, how can I be sure Olivia is really your sister? Until she says so, I'm not moving anything."

Brad eyed him warily. "Tell him who I am, Liv."

She looked from Owen to her brother and back. "I never saw the man before in my life."

"She's your sister, all right," Owen said dryly, withdrawing his hand in a slow caress of her shoulder as Brad bit back the oath he'd been about to let go. "Olivia would never waste her abuse on someone she didn't love."

Olivia could tell Brad still wasn't sure if he'd won or lost that round, or what to make of the tall, muscled tough guy he'd caught pawing his little sister. The fact that the nurse had helped her clean up and he was still wearing several shades of dirt and grime probably didn't help him decide.

She decided the best place to start smoothing the waters between the two men was with an introduction. After they'd shaken hands, with an undercurrent of reservation on Brad's part and amusement on Owen's, she explained to her brother what had happened. In turn, he told them that he'd learned she was in the hospital from one of the diehards still partying at Owen's place.

"Did anyone there bother to tell you that I was perfectly fine? And that it is ridiculous for me to be kept in a hospital overnight? For observation,'' she drawled disgustedly.

"It's standard procedure for exposure victims," Owen told Brad.

"Victim?" she echoed. "I am not a victim."

"How long was she out there?" inquired Brad.

"A few hours. The temperature never went below freezing, but it was plenty cold just the same, and wet. And she wasn't dressed appropriately."

"I'm not surprised," said Brad. "My mother's always nagging her to wear a hat, but she's more concerned about her hair than catching pneumonia."

"Stubborn," pronounced Owen.

"You said it."

Olivia fumed as they continued to talk over her, sparing her only an occasional disapproving glance.

"If you medical experts are through discussing my case," she ventured when there was a pause, "I wonder if the two of you would do something for me?"

"Sure."

Owen nodded.

"Get the hell out of my room."

They laughed.

"Don't you dare laugh at me," she said.

They tried to stop.

"All right, stay if you insist. But you have to start talking *to* me, not *about* me and *over* me."

"She's right," said Owen.

"I suppose," Brad agreed.

"Listen to yourselves. You're doing it again already."

Fighting a grin, Owen reached behind her. "You want undivided attention, you've got it. Let me fluff your pillow for you, sweetheart." He pulled it from under her and punched it a few times. "Much better. Sit up."

"I can't," she retorted. "I think I sprained my neck when you jerked the pillow away."

"Look on the bright side," he urged, effortlessly pulling her forward with one hand while he dropped the pillow behind her with the other. "Now you have a reason to be here."

"Gosh, how can I ever thank you?"

He pretended to think. "Would you consider a vow of silence?"

"I'd be happy to. Of course, I'll miss the sound of your voice barking orders at me, but if it's what you want…" She let the remark trail off with an accommodating little shrug.

Brad had quietly repositioned himself across the bed, where he could observe both of them serve and volley. From the corner of her eye Olivia noticed he was watching with the same fascination he would the Wimbledon finals.

"So how long have you two been in love?" he asked at the first chance they gave him.

Olivia shot her brother a warning look. The last thing she needed was family piling on just when Owen's staunch refusal to admit his feelings seemed to be softening a little. Unless he was being nice because he felt sorry for her. Either way, brotherly interference wasn't likely to help.

"Really, Brad, what an absurd question to ask."

"If it's so absurd, why doesn't one of you answer it?"

"I'll answer the question," said Owen.

She made a calming motion in his direction. "I'll

handle this.'' To Brad she showed clenched teeth and said, ''We are not in love.''

''Yes, we are,'' insisted Owen.

Olivia's heart lurched, with panic, with disbelief, with hope. ''We're really not.''

''We really are. I want to marry your sister.''

''You don't.'' She hadn't meant to whisper.

''I do.''

''So you want to marry her. What does my sister want?'' Brad was clearly enjoying himself no end.

''The same, I think.'' He reached for her hand and clasped it between his. ''We're currently in negotiation.''

''We're no such thing.''

''Sure we are.''

''I thought anything more serious than—'' She caught herself, remembering Brad just in time. ''Dating. I thought anything more than *dating* was nonnegotiable.''

''You were wrong. So was I. Dating has been—'' his eyes warmed, then went hot ''—spectacular. But I want more, much more than a *date* from you, Olivia.''

Her heart swelled. Her eyes watered. ''I don't think I can think.''

''There's nothing to think about,'' he told her with the easy confidence of a man who's stopped hiding. ''It's settled.''

''Nothing is settled.''

''Everything is settled. I surrender. Fully. Forever.''

''Damn,'' muttered Brad as Olivia tried to breathe. He shook his head at Owen. ''You were doing so well for a while there. I really thought you had a handle on her. Then that word.'' He shivered. ''Surrender. You can't surrender to a woman like Olivia.''

"I call them like I see them," said Owen, watching her. When her eyes brightened, letting him know she also remembered the night she'd said the same thing to him. The memory spun out between them, real though unspoken. It was a single thread, winding its way through the invisible, unbreakable threads that already bound them together, leaving room for all the threads waiting ahead to be spun.

"Are you crying, Liv?" Her brother sounded torn between concern and astonishment.

"Of course I'm crying. This is the most romantic moment of my life."

Brad looked around the stark white room and at the grungy looking guy holding hands with Olivia and looking at her with more honest emotion than all the countless men who'd preceded him put together. "Okay. I'm not sure I'd go as far as romantic, but you're the expert." He shifted awkwardly as her tears threatened to spill over. He looked to Owen to share his discomfiture and saw nothing even close. He was definitely the outsider here. He grinned. "I think this is the part where I get to ask if your intentions toward my sister are honorable."

"No," replied Owen. "This is the part where you get to leave."

"Never let it be said I missed a cue." He leaned over to kiss Olivia's cheek, throwing in a private wink of approval for good measure. Olivia was glad for it. She didn't need her family's seal of approval to know she was right about Owen, but it was a bonus to have her brother's gut instinct confirm her own.

With Brad gone, Owen dragged a chair from across the room to sit as close to her as he could get. He reclaimed her hand, carried it to his lips and kissed it, and said the last thing she expected to hear.

"I'm sorry you missed out on the final round at Sugar's."

She'd forgotten all about Sugar's and the contest. Even now that he'd reminded her, all that seemed very faraway and fuzzy, the way the edges of a film get when the director wants to focus the audience's attention on one particular spot. Olivia's focus was entirely on this moment and this man.

"It's not a big deal," she assured him. "Right now it hurts just to *think* about dancing around on a stage. I may have to retire the act."

"I thought hearing that would make me happy. It doesn't."

"Because you feel sorry for me?"

He shook his head. "Because I want to support everything you do, and everything you ever dream of doing. I should have been doing that all along. I never want to hold you back or try to control you."

"I wouldn't let you, anyway."

He grinned. "I know. That was the first thing that got me thinking I was wrong and you were right. About everything. When I saw you tossing that dinner in the trash, I knew you were the woman for me."

"You did, huh?"

He nodded. "I didn't know for sure until I was driving away afterward. I've never felt that lousy. That sorry. I wanted to go back. I thought of about a thousand things I should have said and wished I'd said, but I never once thought about washing the pain away with a few drinks. That's what my father would have done. 'Nothing a bottle of scotch won't cure,' that was his motto. I'm not my father. I never will be."

Her lips curved gently at the trace of wonder in his voice, as he was still getting used to the idea. "I know."

"So do I now. You were right. I was afraid. I just couldn't admit it. You were right about that, too." He looked more relaxed than she had seen him. The fear and tension and ugliness gone, or relegated to the past where they belonged.

"The crazy thing is that I couldn't admit I was afraid of loving you and letting you love me, until I separated my weaknesses from my father's. I'd always believed they were one and the same."

"I love your weaknesses, whatever they are."

"I'm sure you'll point them out as they rear their ugly heads."

She dipped her head and kissed the backs of his hands, one, then the other.

"Of course, as soon as I got rid of one fear, I got blindsided by another one. One that makes the last one a walk in the park." He brushed the hair from the side of her face and rested his hand on her cheek. "When I was out there looking for you, I found out that my fear of loving you was nothing compared to the fear of losing you. I don't think I can shake this one, sweetheart. I don't think I want to if it helps me remember how much I treasure you."

"Stop," she begged, freeing her hand so she could wind her arms around his neck. She wanted her body pressed to his, all of hers against all of his. This was a start. "Kiss me. Before I hyperventilate."

He tipped her head back and opened his mouth over hers in a kiss that was long and deep and wonderful.

"Again," she murmured against his lips.

"In a minute," he promised, heat and laughter tangled in his voice. "There's something else you have to know about me. It's complicated. Too complicated to figure out right now. We come from different worlds.''

"We can work all that out.''

"I know. This is something else. About me. Your brother seems like a decent guy, but he's just exactly like I imagined he would be. Everything I'm not. Everything I'll never be. I'm not slick.''

"I don't want slick.''

"Or driven...at least not in that corporate, thousand-dollar-suit way.''

"I don't want driven or suits.''

"Good, because you won't get them from me. I won't ever be some kind of ornament. I'm not a pretty boy.''

"No, darling, you are most definitely not pretty. You are, however, big and rough and sexy. And mine.''

"That's another thing.''

"Are there many more?'' she asked, impatient to hold him, touch him, before the nurse remembered he was there and threw him out.

"Last one,'' he promised. "The most important. You need to know this because it's not ever going to change, no matter what you say or do.'' She braced herself. "You need to know I love you. Because I do. I think I always have. I know I'll never stop. I love you, Olivia.''

"Say it again.''

"I love you, Olivia. Marry me, Olivia,'' he scattered kisses along her throat for punctuation. "Come and live with me and my dogs, burn my dinner, dump my files, for better or worse, forever.''

"There are a few conditions.''

"Name them.''

"I want babies. And family vacations. And a carpool. But not a minivan.''

''Babies, vacations, carpool, but no minivan. I can handle all that. And I want to start on the babies first.''

''I was hoping you'd say that. Because I want to start now.''

* * * * *

SILHOUETTE®
SPECIAL EDITION™

AVAILABLE FROM 17TH OCTOBER 2003

GOOD HUSBAND MATERIAL Susan Mallery
Hometown Heartbreakers

When Kari Asbury revisited her home town she never expected to bump into ex-fiancé Sheriff Gage Reynolds. But could Kari find the courage to overcome their past and stand by the man she'd always loved?

TALL, DARK AND IRRESISTIBLE Joan Elliott Pickart
The Baby Bet: MacAllister's Gifts

Ryan Sharpe was blatantly masculine, sexy and…irresistible. He could be with anyone, but his passionate pursuit told Carolyn he wanted *only* her. Dare Carolyn believe he'd still want her when he learned her secret?

MY SECRET WIFE Cathy Gillen Thacker
The Deveraux Legacy

A secret sex-only marriage was the only way Dr Gabe Deveraux knew to help best friend Maggie Calloway have a baby. But soon Gabe was forced to admit the truth—he'd secretly loved Maggie for years.

AN AMERICAN PRINCESS Tracy Sinclair

When Shannon Blanchard won TV's hottest game show, she never dreamed that her prize of two weeks at a royal castle would change her life. Until she set eyes on tall, dark and dangerously attractive Prince Michel de Mornay…

LT KENT: LONE WOLF Judith Lyons

Journalist Angie Rose wanted to unveil the hero…the mysterious millionaire that was Lt Jason Kent. But how could she expose Jason's secrets when their passion—*her heart*—revealed they were meant to be together?

THE STRANGER SHE MARRIED Crystal Green
Kane's Crossing

Two years ago Rachel Shane's husband vanished. Then, without warning, a rugged stranger with familiar eyes sauntered into her life professing amnesia. He was *all*-male and every inch a dangerous temptation…

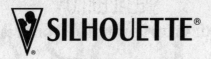

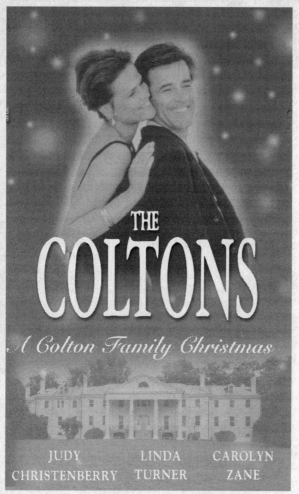

THE COLTONS

A Colton Family Christmas

JUDY
CHRISTENBERRY

LINDA
TURNER

CAROLYN
ZANE

On sale 17th October 2003

*Available at most branches of WHSmith,
Tesco, Martins, Borders, Eason, Sainsbury's
and all good paperback bookshops.*

4 FREE

books and a surprise gift!

We would like to take this opportunity to thank you for reading th
Silhouette® book by offering you the chance to take FOUR mo
specially selected titles from the Special Edition™ series absolute
FREE! We're also making this offer to introduce you to the benefi
of the Reader Service™—

- ★ FREE home delivery
- ★ FREE gifts and competitions
- ★ FREE monthly Newsletter
- ★ Exclusive Reader Service discount
- ★ Books available before they're in the shops

Accepting these FREE books and gift places you under n
obligation to buy, you may cancel at any time, even after receivir
your free shipment. Simply complete your details below and retur
the entire page to the address below. *You don't even need a stamp.*

YES! Please send me 4 free Special Edition books and a surpri
gift. I understand that unless you hear from me, I will receiv
6 superb new titles every month for just £2.90 each, postage ar
packing free. I am under no obligation to purchase any books ar
may cancel my subscription at any time. The free books and gift w
be mine to keep in any case.

E3Z

Ms/Mrs/Miss/Mr ....Initials................................
BLOCK CAPITALS PLEA

Surname ....

Address ....

....

....Postcode..................................

Send this whole page to:
UK: FREEPOST CN81, Croydon, CR9 3WZ
EIRE: PO Box 4546, Kilcock, County Kildare (stamp required)